JAMES Y. BARTLETT

Death from the Ladies Tee

A HACKER MYSTERY

YEOMAN HOUSE

To my mother
And to her sisters, all of whom have managed their
lives -- and golf games -- with grace and style, unflag-
ging good humor and boundless enthusiasm.

Three things there are as unfathomable as they are fascinating
to the masculine mind: metaphysics, golf, and the feminine heart.

--Arnold Haultain, *The Mystery of Golf*

Golf may be a sophisticated game. At least, it is usually played
with the outward appearance of great dignity. It is, neverthe-
less, a game of considerable passion, either of the explosive
type, or that which burns inwardly and sears the soul.

--Bob Jones

ONE

S *on-of-a-bitchin' mother-fuckin' shit-eatin' puke!"*

I am ashamed to say that those were the first words my new neighbor heard me utter. It was a gloriously warm and sunny day in late April on Boston's North Shore, and I scored a direct hit, hammer upon thumb, just as the tall and somewhat gangly woman strode confidently around the corner of my beach shack.

I performed the cartoonesque dance of pain, leaping about furiously, shaking the throbbing digit, then cramming it into my mouth for a soothing suck, until I finally noticed her standing there. Her eyes had widened perceptibly. Her lips were pursed in an unsuccessful attempt to avoid smiling at my misfortune.

"Oh dear," she said, trying not to laugh. "I should expect that would smart." Her voice was plumy and clipped just this side of pseudo-British. Her mousy brown hair was pulled back off her face and tied in a proper bun. She was tall with broad shoulders and long, thin arms that contributed to her gangly image. Although thin, she was still properly curved. She was dressed in a sleeveless blouse and shorts, but had a sensible cable-knit sweater knotted around her shoulders. I try hard not to typecast people, especially ones I've only just met, but my inner filter immediately registered: "Cambridge...professor ... spinster-to-be."

"'Scuse me," I mumbled, thumb still in mouth.

"Quite all right, done it many a time myself," she said forcefully. She reached out, grabbed my unhurt hand and began pumping it up and down with vigor.

"Moira Daughtry," she introduced herself. "My friends call me 'Mo.' We're to be neighbors this summer. Here, let me."

She picked up my hammer where I had dropped it, steadied the shutter I had been holding and drove the nail home in one firm, inerrant blow, securing it in place.

It was my vacation. I always take the better part of a month off in late April and early May. Exactly one week ago, I had been down in Augusta, Georgia to witness "the Dashing Scot," Ian MacDuff, capture the hallowed Masters with a sterling back nine on another historic Sunday afternoon at the National. Because I had been on the road almost constantly for the six weeks of the Tour swing through Florida, and because there are no really important tournaments on the schedule until the U.S. Open in June, my editor agrees to give me some time off post-Masters. I would head back out on the road in the middle of May, which was about when the top players would begin to focus their intensity on the upcoming national championship.

As I do almost every year, I was spending my off time trying to get my beach house in shape for the season. It's not much of a house – really just a shack – but it's one of my proudest possessions. It had belonged to my Uncle Charles, a dedicated and lifelong bachelor and globe-trotting oil company executive who had left me the house to use as he had: as a brief but treasured escape from the ordinary world.

The house is located out on an isolated spit of land called Cross Banks overlooking Ipswitch Bay, about thirty-five miles north of Boston. There are maybe a dozen shacks like mine on this bluff, protected at the rear by a few hundred acres of marshland. From our narrow strip, the dunes run down to a rocky beach. As you face the bay, off to the left is the Plum Island bird sanctuary, and across a broad tidal cut to the right is Crane's Beach.

Uncle Charley had not been able to use the house much more than I could. But I like to spend a few spring weeks out there, repairing winter damage, preparing for the summer onslaught, and enjoying the peace, quiet and emptiness of the place. I try to come back for a week in September, when the summer beach crowds have gone back home, and the golden tones of the autumn sun wash over the gloriously clean and empty beaches. During the summer, while I am off covering the victories and defeats of the weekly PGA Tour events for the Boston *Journal*, various relatives sign up for week-long visits. I rent the place out, only to those I know well, the rest of the summer. Frankly, I don't know how the families who pile in stand the place. It's tiny, just two bedrooms, a bathroom with shower stall, tiny kitchenette, and living room and deck facing the sea. It's just right for me, but it must be hideously cramped, noisy and smelly for families with more than two members.

Anyway, the neighborly Mo Daughtry finished nailing up the shutter supports along the south wall with professional aplomb. While I nursed my thumb, she chattered away all the while about her own adjacent shack, which she was renting from a very good friend in the English Department for the summer, how much she admired the view and how she hoped before summer's end to stage a genuine New England clambake down on the beach and would I be interested in helping?

I explained to her gently that I would only be on site for a week or two.

I could see her face fall. She had apparently been measuring me out for a relationship suit.

"And what is your occupation, er, Mister …?" she asked graciously.

"Hacker," I said. "Pete Hacker. I write for the Boston *Journal.*"

"Indeed?" she said. "A journalist!" She brightened. I could almost see the mental tape measure come slinging out.

"Well, not quite," I said. "I'm a sportswriter. I cover the professional golf tour."

"Ah," she said, eyes clouding again. Apparently, her circle in the English Department was not made up of avid golfers. Then she perked up again. "My uncle played golf," she said brightly. "Winston Butterfield was his name. Do you know of him?"

"Gosh," I said, "I don't think that I do. Of course, there are only twenty-five million golfers in this country. Maybe I just haven't crossed paths with him yet."

Okay, perhaps I sounded a little peevish. But this damn woman was getting on my nerves. Not that I minded her carpentry skills. Still, I come to the beach to get away from people, not to socialize.

She got my drift.

"Of course," she said. "How silly of me. Well, it has been a pleasure meeting you. I do hope to see you and Mrs. Hacker at some point this summer."

"There is no Mrs. Hacker," I told her, wishing immediately that I hadn't.

"Indeed?" she said, sizing me up again. Her tone said "Inseam: very good."

"Well then, toodle-oo!" She gave a wave and disappeared around the side of my house, as quickly and silently as she had appeared. Toodle-oo. I don't think anyone had ever actually said that to me before in my entire life. Toodle-oo.

I got the cold sweats just thinking about it.

TWO

I wisely decided to postpone the rest of my planned renovation activities until the next day. The shutter project and the new screen for the front door could wait until Monday.

There were maybe two good hours of sun left in the afternoon, and in Boston in late April one learns to treasure warm sun. I threw on an old sweater, poured myself a healthy Dewar's on the rocks, grabbed a thick book on English history, and went out to the deck. I figured to use the sweater and the Scotch to scientifically counteract the steady diminution of the sun's warmth as it set behind me. After an hour or so, I got up and refilled the glass. All in the interest of science, of course. A line of low, scudding clouds had blown up and I could feel the temperature begin to drop as the wind shifted around to come off the ocean. Tomorrow looked like it might be cloudy and rainy. "Darn," I thought facetiously, "might have to postpone those damn shutters for another day."

My telephone rang just as I decided to call it an afternoon. Coincidentally, my second Scotch was about gone. I went inside and answered it.

"Hacker, is that you?" a cheerful female voice asked. "God, I can't believe what a pain in the ass it has been to track you down! You'll never guess who this is!"

She was young, I could tell, and she sounded vaguely familiar. But she was right…I couldn't quite place her.

"I give up," I said.

"Honie Carlton!" she exclaimed. "Remember me?"

I immediately felt old and I think five more hairs on my head switched over to gray. Honie Carlton had been a neighbor child back home in Wallingford. When I had left home to seek fame and fortune, she had been barely in her teens. The girl who lived Two Doors Down. Over the years, she and my parents had become close. They took an interest in her and she adopted them. Backed goods and gossip passed across the fence developed into an abiding love. I would always hear about her progress in school during my intermittent visits home. At Thanksgiving or Christmas she would sometimes drop in for a dram of holiday cheer. A pretty young thing, every year growing into her female gracefulness. Last report I had heard, a few years ago, was that she was in college and studying marketing.

"Honie Carlton," I said. "You sound all growed up. How *did* you find me?"

She laughed in delight – a clear, self-satisfied, tinkling laugh.

"Well, I started by calling New Orleans, where I thought you'd be covering the Tour," she said. "I talked to some guy down there named Corcoran, who said he didn't know where in the hell you were."

"That's Billy, the information officer," I told her. "You should have talked to his assistant, Suzy. She knows more than Billy ever forgot, which is a lot."

"Well, then I called the sports desk at the Journal, but whoever answered said you were probably down in New Orleans, ummm, 'banging some golf groupies' was the way he put it, I think." She laughed again.

I was too embarrassed to respond. The Honie I remembered had been such an innocent, clean-cut child.

"Then, " she continued, "I did what I shoulda done first. I called your old man. He said you were on vacation and probably out fixing up your beach shack. He gave me the number. And here you are!"

"Well, damn," I said. "You get the gold metal for perseverance. What are you up to these days? Last I heard you were in college somewhere."

"I graduated in December," she said. "And after looking around and interviewing all over the damn place, I got a job two months ago."

"Which is …"

"Information officer for the Ladies' Professional Golf Tour," she said proudly.

"Aha," I said.

"Oh, Hacker, now don't be that way," she said quickly. "I'm not calling to hustle you. Well, I guess I am, kinda, but not …"

I chuckled. "Just yanking your chain, kid," I said. "Congratulations. That's a great job, especially for a young kid just out of college. And God knows they need the help."

The LPGA, although more than 50 years old, is always struggling, it seems, for financial support, a fan base, publicity, TV time. For whatever reason, the ladies' tour just cannot quite get over the hump.

"But I thought you were majoring in marketing," I said.

"Yeah, this is kind of the first step," she said. "You see, what this tour needs is marketing and exposure. I'm working the exposure end right now, and I'm in line to move into marketing in another year or two."

"I didn't know you were a golfer," I said.

"Oh, hell, Hacker," she laughed. "I don't know a three-wood from a sand wedge. But my job isn't to play this silly game. Just to get it into the public's mind."

"And how are you doing?" I asked, knowing I shouldn't.

"Well,"she said coyly. "That's one reason I'm calling."

"The other reason being, of course, you couldn't wait to catch up on old news from an old someone you probably remember not at all."

"You're right, Hacker," she laughed. "Except I do remember you. But business is business and you're the best golf writer I know. Hell, the *only* golf writer I know! I thought, at the last, you could give me some advice ..." She trailed off hopefully.

"Put out plenty of cold beer and coldcuts," I suggested. "The press will come running to do your bidding."

She laughed, saying "Oh, Hacker! But seriously, we don't get much coverage for some reason. I mean, we're supposed to be an established sports organization and we can't get into the newspapers on a regular basis. I mean, the golf newspapers do OK, and the AP and local media show up for events, but we're always an afterthought. It's really too bad, because these girls can really play."

"I don't know why, either," I said. "At first blush, you could say the great American public doesn't go for women's professional sports. But then you think about tennis, and the women there seem to be able to pack 'em in. And figure skating, skiing, women's soccer … all do pretty good."

"Exposure is the key," Honie agreed. "We're trying real hard to get more of our tournaments on television, but in the meantime, I've got to try and recruit more print media attention. Which is why I thought of you," she said primly.

"Honie –" I started.

"I mean, you're not busy with the men's tour right now…"

"Honie –"

"And we're in the middle of our Florida swing, and the weather's real nice down here …"

"Honie –"

"And it would really make me some Brownie points with my boss …"

"Honie –"

"And I can get you a free hotel room and interviews with anyone you want. We've got a real strong field this week, and …"

"Honie –"

"What do you think? Will you come down?"

I used to think they taught Hounding to women in college: Perseverance 101. But now I'm beginning to think it's just a natural, inborn trait of the species.

"Honie, it's my time off," I said gently. "I don't want to work. I want to putter around here and bang my thumb with the hammer and read six good books I've been saving and drink a lot of Scotch and watch the waves crash against the rocks over there." I stopped because I think I was starting to whine. That's not good. Whining shows weakness. Women like weakness and know how to exploit it.

"Oh, that's all right, Hacker," Honie said. "I just thought you might like to spend a week down here in Miami. Did I mention that we're playing at the Doral this weekend? I could get you a suite, I think. But if you'd rather not, I understand. I guess." She tried unsuccessfully to keep the disappointment out of her voice.

The great Bobby Jones used to say he believed that the results of every tournament he ever played were determined in advance by some great Divine Providence before anyone teed off, and that all he and his fellow competitors were doing was playing out the predetermined Will of said Providence.

I think the Divine P wanted me in Miami, because just at that moment, I saw Mo Daughtry come striding toward the front door of my cottage. In the fading twilight, I saw that she was carrying a bottle of something…sherry, I guessed…and two glasses.

"Yoo-hoo, Peter!" she chirruped from the doorway. "I find myself in need of a corkscrew. Have you one handy?"

The yoo-hoo got me. So did the Peter. No one called me Peter. But so did the sudden clarity with which I saw my predicament. The two glasses were the tip-off. My corkscrew would lead to her offer of a neighborly sherry in thanks.

And then two or three more. She would be liberal with the refilling. That would lead to slightly slurred words, batted eyes, casual caress, shy giggles and a sudden, more meaningful glance. There would be a sudden attack with her hot, slack mouth, hoping that the three, or was it four, sherries would have broken down any remaining resistance and inhibition. There would be a frantic shedding of clothes, the rapid unveiling of that knobbly body with her broad shoulders and sharp angles and its pale white of desperation. But after three, or was it four?, sherries, who cares? And then would come the rushing, gasping, frantic chase, faster and harder. Bony hips digging into thighs. Release, oblivion, collapse. Until the morning, or an hour or so later, when the time would come to sort out the emotions and determine the question of "what's next" in the cold and harsh light of daybreak.

And even if I were able to somehow avoid that scenario tonight, tomorrow would bring another attack, a different strategy, a ratcheting up of the siege.

"Honie," I said into the phone, "I've changed my mind. Miami sounds great. I'll be down tomorrow afternoon."

"Oh, Hacker…thanks!" she exclaimed. "You are a prince! There's a flight from Boston at two that gets in at five-thirty. I'll meet you."

I thought about this for a second. "How did you know what time the flights were?" I wondered. "That's … that's …" I cast about for just the right epithet to hurl at her across the telephone.

"Professional," she said. "Very professional."

THREE

O n the plane ride down to Miami the next afternoon, I thought about the LPGA. It was true that the ladies' game did not receive the same attention as the men's. Except for the one week each summer when the women played a tournament in greater Boston, and another week when the U.S. Golf Association held their national Open for women, news about women's golf was buried deep inside the Journal's sports pages, right next to the bowling league scores.

Something didn't add up. The women's professional tour had been around since the 1940s, and there had been a steady progression of excellent women players over the years: Babe Didrickson, Patty Berg, Mickey Wright, Kathy Whitworth, JoAnne Carner, Wynnona Stilwell, and in recent years, Nancy

Lopez, Pat Bradley, Betsy King, Beth Daniel, Patty Sheehan, Annika Sorenstam and many others.

So it certainly wasn't a lack of marquee names that held the tour back as a successful enterprise. Nor did it seem the tour was lacking a fan base. I had recently read some statistics that showed the numbers of women golfers in the United States had reached more than twenty-five percent of the total and was climbing steadily every year. I knew from personal experience that more and more women were playing the game. You saw them everywhere. And they had won important battles for equality at private clubs all across the country.

But the LPGA continued to struggle, year after year. Struggled for tournament sponsors, struggled to fill up every week with another event, struggled for face time on TV. Even the men's senior tour, made up of fat, paunchy and graying men well past their prime, had been organized out of nowhere and rocketed to success. The old guys had no trouble finding sponsors, filling weekends and getting TV time. It didn't seem fair, somehow.

Why was the LPGA having so much trouble attracting attention and dollars? The modern era of the tour had been plagued by a series of terrible leaders whose mismanagement had saddled the organization with some heavy credibility problems among the powers-that-be, both at the network and corporate levels. And it was widely believed that women professionals, even on shortened courses, don't make enough birdies to satisfy a rabid fan. This, I knew, was a subjective opinion, but held more than a grain of truth. While women pros have beautiful swings and all the abilities and shotmaking skills, they do not usually perform with the same kind of bravura, knock-down-the-pins attitudes witnessed every weekend on the men's tour. At least, that's the common perception. And it needs to be overcome.

Further, I mused as the plane throbbed its way south over an unending back of blue-gray clouds, the current women's tour had not developed a lot of distincntive personalities at the top. I cringed in my seat as imaginary shrews began shrieking protests at me. *What about Betsy King?* they yelled. *What about Annika? Nancy Lopez? Karrie Webb? How can you say such a thing?*

I could say it because it was true. Nancy Lopez had certainly excited lots of attention in her deyday, especially 1978, the year she won five tournaments in a row. But these days, with three kids in tow, Nancy's best golf is behind her. Betsy King? A dominating player for a while, but as exciting to watch as a Swiss cheese. Annika has certainly perked up the impressions people have of women golfers, and deservedly so, but who competes with her? Karrie Webb did for a while, and then faded. And Webb fell into the category of women golfers who are certainly accomplished golfers, but whose personalities and appearance don't seem to appeal to an admittedly sexist American sporting public. It's the Anna Kournakova syndrome: If you look gorgeous, attention will follow you, even if you can't play a lick. But you can be a worldbeater, and if you're a bit zaftig or if you play with a scowl or if you don't resemble the perennial girl next door, no one will care. Unfair? Unquestionably. Fixable? Probably not in this lifetime.

And, of course, the LPGA had what we all euphemistically called the "image problem." There had always been whispering about the "image problem." Some of my more cynical golf writer associates had a different phrase: "dykes in spikes."

Also unfair, the LPGA had long battled the perception that most of its players were lesbians. No one that I know had ever taken a survey, and the LPGA's own press manual did not list the sexual inclinations of the players. But whenever the subject of the LPGA came up, in boozy late-night bar conversations, or in coded references in published stories, the lesbian thing always came up. We writers often gossiped or exchanged info on what we'd heard. That the winner of three major tournaments whose constant travel companion always gets a decidedly nonsisterly smooch after every good round. The leading money winner who likes to cruise the leather bars in each city she visits. The new, younger players who get treated like "fresh meat" by the older, experienced pros.

I had listened to, laughed at, and clucked over all these stories over the years. And while it never particularly mattered to me who was sleeping with whom, it figured that some element of homophobia figured into the LPGA's problems. They had always tried to promote their good-looking players – like Laura Baugh and Jan Stevenson – while keeping some of the more mannish types well under wraps. It was grossly unfair, but the LPGA had to market itself toward the heterosexual ideal: blond, good-looking and fresh. The PGA Tour didn't have those problems. And it was generally assumed that all the male professionals were constantly fending off – or not – women everywhere they went. Another heterosexual ideal.

The shape and substance of my piece began to take some shape as I thought about these things. Perhaps I could send it over to our Sunday magazine, and made a mental note to contact that editor to talk it over with him. The readers of the Boston Journal's sports pages are probably more comfortable with Red Sox box scores than with the sexual identity of the woman golfer.

Honie Carlton was waiting for me when I deplaned in the humidity of Miami. I almost didn't recognize her. She had indeed grown up. The pert and cheerful little teenager I remembered had become a stunning young woman with all the requisite curves and shapes that entails. She was wearing a soft pink sleeveless top and a conservative but shapely white skirt. Her light brown hair was pulled back from her face and tied with a pink bow, and some cheerfully colored earrings jiggled with the movement of her head. Her pale blue eyes were alight in her perfect face, soft round lips tinged with just the slightest shade of pink.

Like any other red-blooded American male, I felt my heart do a quick flip-flop as I studied her. But then I imaged what my mother would say to such thoughts, and quickly pushed them aside.

"Hacker!" she cried as she came running up and gave me a big hug. "Jeez, it's so good to see you! Thanks so much for coming down."

"God, child, you make me feel old before my time," I said, slinging my leather carryall over my shoulder and trying not to walk stooped over. She frowned at me prettily.

"When people say things like that to me, it makes me feel like I'm fourteen and trying on my first training bra," she pouted.

"You're right," I said. "I apologize. It's always difficult for one generation to admit the next to all the privileges of adulthood."

"Whoa," she said. "That's deep." She giggled.

We made small talk as we collected my bags, walked outside into a thick vapor of humidity and piled into a cab. Miami is probably my least favorite city in probably my least favorite state. Never mind the constant heat that always saps whatever reserves if strength I have built up; never mind the little bugs that seem to find me, no matter how far indoors I take myself or how thickly I lather myself with dope; never mind that the golf courses —uniformly flat, watery and breezy—all seem to run together in my head after a while.

No, what I don't like about Miami in particular and Florida in general, is the built-in isolation. There are no neighborhoods in Florida … only walled compounds. Except for the slums and barrios. There are no homes with yards in Miami, just impregnable villas surrounded by tall stucc walls and screened-in swimming pools. Miami, the sun-and-fun capital of the world, is really an indoor place: hidden, private, secret and usually off-limits. Air-conditioned and kept cool and dark. Protected by private cops in gatehouses, security patrols, angry dogs and DO NOT ENTER signs.

Maybe they've got it right and the rest of us are wrong. The world is a dangerous place. Carving out a private and hidden sanctuary and not letting anyone in without prior clearance is perhaps the best way to combat that danger. But as an outsider, Miami always makes me feel uneasy. A trespasser in paradise.

From the airport, our cab rode us past a few of those walled paradises and through a section of slum before pulling swiftly through the enormous stucco gate that marks the entrance to the Doral Golf Resort & Spa. We moved from the hot, simmering asphalt streets into a whisper-quiet, lushly landscaped tropical setting, with towering royal palms, expansively huge banana trees, flowering hibiscus and oleander, and acres of well-tended beds of coleus and marigolds. Fountains gushed from the center of lakes. A strong, athletic girl in a swimsuit of spun gold hurled herself from a a high-dive platform into a sparkling pool. Tennis was being played by matrons dressed in crisp whites. And from the winding drive, I saw glimpses, too, of green and manicured fairways across which drove gold-colored golf carts whose roofs were fringed in white.

The cab pulled up to the imposing entrance lobby, where a tall and muscular black man, dressed in some absurd kind of English colonial military uniform, right down to the white pith helmet piped in gold braid, waved us to a stop. With military precision, he lifted my suitcase out of the trunk, waved the cab on and pointed the way to the registration desk.

"Welcome to the Doral," he said. "Please enjoy your stay."

He did not call me Bwana, which was a disappointment.

"Sim salla bim," I said to him and handed him a couple of bucks.

"I beg your pardon?" he said. I noticed his gold-plated name tag said CARL. So much for colonial authenticity.

With Honie hovering about helpfully, I checked in. She had arranged a junior suite for me, which typically runs about $350 a night. The desk clerk passed over the registration form for me to sign. I noticed that in the block headed "Room

Rate" it said "Complimentary, $0.00." All hail the power of the press.

We were assigned a bellman and went back outside to collect my bag. Just as we reached the curb, a gigantic black limo pulled in. Do they make stretch Bentleys? This monster had rolling black fenders, some strange kind of sterling silver hood ornament, oversized whitewalls, glistening grillwork and tinted windows. It looked like it was twenty-five feet long.

I felt Honie come to attention beside me. Carl leaped to open the rear door and, with an extra flourish, extended his white-gloved hand inside to aid the passenger's disembarkation.

Out of the car came Wynnona Haybrook Stilwell. She was one of the LPGA's few instantly recognizable celebrities. Wyn Haybrook had been one of America's finest amateur players as a teen. Tall, big-boned and rangy, she had carved an impressive path through the golf tournaments of her day. She had played a power game that few other women possessed. She could boom her driver miles down the fairway, hit crisp and precise iron shots and sink putts from anywhere. And it was as a youth that she got tagged with her nickname. It was the newspapers that created it. "Another Big Wyn for Haybrook." "Big Wyn Does It Again." "Ladies Open: A Big Wyn in a Rout."

When she turned pro, Big Wyn kept on winning, both as Haybrook and later as Mrs. Stilwell. She was one of the Big Three in the women's game, along with Kathy Whitworth and JoAnne Carner. It was the distaff version of Palmer, Nicklaus and Player.

While, as with the other two, her heyday had largely passed, she was still considered a dangerous golfer – always capable of throwing up a low number on any given day. And Big Wyn continued to dominate the ladies' tour in other ways. For more than ten years, she had been president of the tour's Player's Association, and was a force in determining how the tour was operated. "Got to look after my girls," she was always quoted as saying.

Big Wyn Stilwell looked more like the Queen Mother than a den mother as she emerged from the limo. She was still tall, but her girth had expanded some over the years. Still, she had an athletic build with broad and powerful-looking shoulders and strong-looking arms. Her skin was the deeply tanned shade of an outdoor person. Her once-golden hair had begun to lighten to gray and she wore it in a tight, short, manly cut, parted on one side.

Her face was the key to her celebrity. Its chiseled features were instantly recognizable. That defiant jut of her jaw, those flashing, angry-looking brown eyes, those strong lips pursed in furious concentration. That was the picture most of us had of Big Wyn as she marched determinedly down the fairway to yet another championship. Even here, on a hot, muggy sidewalk, one could look at BigWyn and hear the echoes of the cheers of the multitudes ringing softly in the breeze.

Once out of the limo, Big Wyn strode purposefully into the hotel without waiting for the rest of her party. Climbing out after her was a small, pale man, balding above the temples, nattily dressed in a dark charcoal suit with tie and matching pocket square. Emerging into the bright Florida sun, he squinted against the light and clutched a briefcase protectively against his chest.

"That's Benton Bergmeister," Honie whispered to me, identifying the commissioner of the LPGA Tour. Bergmeister caught sight of Big Wyn's stern disappearing into the hotel and set out at a half-trot to catch up with her. It reminded me of the White Rabbit scurrying after the Queen of Hearts.

Last one out of the limo was one of those rare creatures — and honest-to-God, heart-in-the-throat, pulse-stopping, head-turning babe.Long, long legs unfolded out of the door, followed by a torso that had seemingly been poured into a shimmering, ice-blue dress that just barely accomplished the business of clothing. And the package was topped, as such a package should be, with faultless blond hair, high cheekbones, sharp blue eyes and pouty lips framed in a long, smooth face.

She emerged as if in slow motion from the limo and stood there a moment, smoothing down her dress over a body that should have been illegal. Carl flashed her a silly smile and bowed. I had the feeling that the world around us was reacting as if in one of those brokerage house commercials. Birds stopped signing, insects stopped buzzing. The high diver froze in midair and golfers halted their swings halfway down.

I made some kind of strange, throaty groaning sound that came out in a rough approximation of "Whozzat?"

Honie sighed the sigh of a woman who knows she's been licked and knows there's not a damn thing she can ever do about it. The package in the ice-blue dress was that good.

"That's Casey Carlyle," she told me resignedly. "She's Big Wyn's, ummm, secretary."

I had to start breathing through my nose. My throat was suddenly rendered inoperable.

Honie looked at me with no small measure of disgust. "Calm down, Hacker," she muttered. "You'll get to meet her in person tonight when you meet Big Wyn. I've got you scheduled for cocktails in Wyn's suite at seven. Casey'll be there."

"Eeeep," I managed.

"But I gotta warn you," she added. "Better men than you have tried and perished with that one. She's reputed to be a real ball-breaker."

"Aaarrp," I squeaked.

Honie sighed again, deeply, took my arm and dragged me off to find my hotel room.

FOUR

Honie left me alone to kill a leisurely hour or so wandering around the grounds of the famed Doral, a place I visited every March for the men's tournament staged on the resort's famed Blue Monster course. A monster it is, too, long and winding and tightly guarded on all sides by sand and water. When the wind is up, it's a great test for the pros, but for mere mortal golfers, it can be so difficult as to stop being fun to play.

But the resort has three other courses, all named after a color. The LPGA would be playing on the Old White, east of the main hotel. Meanwhile, the resort's guests could still play the Blue Monster, or the Red or Gold courses, both of which were similar in topography, but surrounded by south Florida housing: tightly packed homes protected by walls. As at many resorts in this modern age of commerce, Doral's big bucks come from conventions and business meetings more than Mom and Pop vacationers. As I wandered around the busy courses in late afternoon, I saw fleets of golf carts set up to handle the crush of business executives who tomorrow would leave a morning seminar and head out en masse to one of the courses for an afternoon of forced sociability. One of Hacker's Rules of Golf, the firmest, is "Never play behind a businessperson's golf group. Instead, head for the nearest bar." This is because most of those forced to play in those afternoon rounds are, at best, twice-a-year golfers who hit the ball sideways with everything up to and usually including the putter. It makes for an excruciating round of golf.

Like most courses in Florida, those at the Doral had a certain sameness: the terrain of monotonous flatness. Golf course architects have labored mightily over the years to break up that monotony by bulldozing the land into mounds and hills, digging out lots of black, murky ponds, framing greens with royal or coconut palms and planting accents of flowering hibiscus or crape myrtle. But whether the holes run straight or dogleg this way or that, there is nothing the architects can do to disguise the basic billiard-table flatness of the land. Nor can they do anything about the hot sun or the fierce mosquitoes. That's golf in Florida.

Still, as I watched the garishly dressed tourists happily flailing away, I realized that this was probably better than, say, Chicago dressed in its late spring coat of cold slushy snow, or Detroit, Buffalo or even my own Boston on a nonwarm April day. Yes, for a day or two of golf, this would do just fine.

I put such philosophical thoughts out of my head by thinking about that vision of loveliness named Casey Carlyle. Returning to my suite, I took a shower, turned on the sports channel and promptly fell asleep.

I put a lot of thought into what to wear for my interview that evening with Casey…er, Big Wyn. I thought about going with the Palm Beach look: pink linen sports coat over some starched white ducks, glistening Gucci loafers. Sockless, of course. It gives the ensemble that extra touch of casual yet studied nonchalance. But it was all fantasy, of course. I am, after all, one of the mastodons of the press box and we have certain standards of our own to maintain. Besides which, I don't own either a pink linen sports coat or a pair of Gucci loafers.

So I dressed in my uniform. Wrinkled khaki trousers. Mostly clean white golf shirt with only one button missing, but what the hell, who buttons golf shirts anyway? My six-year-old navy blue blazer, which is only a little frayed at the cuffs and getting a tad thin at the elbow. Comes from leaning on lots of bars. And, of course, Bass loafers. I left the socks off…when in Rome etc. Looking in the mirror, I saw that I was the veritable picture of studied nonchalance.

Honie came and got me promptly at seven. I was trying to brush my hair back into an insouciant flip when she knocked. She came in and perched on the end of the bed while I fussed in the mirror, watching me with a bemused grin.

"So," I said, studiously nonchalant, trying to keep my voice level and deep. "Tell me something about her." She knew who I meant, of course, and her grin widened. I wasn't paying attention, as I had that last lock of hair just where I wanted it. Kind of the young Marlon Brando meets Tom Cruise. Devastating.

"Okay," Honie finally said with a giggle. "For starters, she sleeps with girls."

I dropped my hairbrush. I stared at Honie to see if she was just pulling my chain. She wasn't. She was laughing her fool head off. I muttered some imprecations. Then I began to swear.

"Tell me, Honie, that there is a God and what you say is not true," I pleaded.

"Sorry, Hacker," she said, wiping her eyes and going off into a fresh bout of laughter. "There are lots of poorly kept secrets in this organization, and that's one of the worst."

"But who? Why?" I was speechless. The waste, the utter waste of it all.

"I'll give you all the soap-opera stuff later," she said, glancing at her watch. "We've got to get over to Big Wyn's suite. She has been known to get pissed if you're late."

She stood up, came over and gave me a peck on the cheek, sisterly like. "Sorry to burst your bubble, but I couldn't let you go make a complete ass of yourself. At least, not on your first night here."

"Thanks a bunch," I grumbled, and we left.

I had thought my junior suite was pretty nice until I saw the penthouse palace occupied by Big Wyn and her party. Honie used a special key in the elevator to whisk us up to the top floor of the hotel. The doors whispered open onto an antechamber done in smoked mirrors and brass-and-crystal chandeliers. We walked down a curved hallway toward the sounds of low conversation and tinkling glasses.

We came out on the balcony level of Wyn's immense suite. The room that lay before us was semicircular, with two-story floor-to-ceiling windows overlooking the golf courses. Beyond were the lights of the downtown Miami skyscrapers, twinkling through the twilight. The room was furnished in Florida elegance: white leather furniture, bright pastel accents, modern art on the walls. It was all just a shade toward the garish. There was a white grand piano, lid propped open. Next to the piano stood a six-foot-tall flower arrangement featuring lots of bright-red corkscrew-like things.

As we stood on the balcony looking over all this opulence, the conversations of the people standing down below gradually stopped. I felt like breaking into the balcony scene from "Romeo and Juliet," but restrained myself for once. Below us, of course, was Big Wyn Stilwell, who was wearing black evening pants and a loose white top. Benton Bergmeister, the LPGA commish, was still wearing his snappy gray suit. He was holding a tall highball glass. Standing over by the window, bedecked in a shimmering red-sequined floor-length dress, all luscious curves and secret shadows, was the lovely and apparently unapproachable Casey Carlyle. I shot her a look of moral disapproval, but I don't think she noticed.

There were two other people in the room I didn't know. One was a short, stocky older gentleman wearing a crisp white overall getup, sort of dress work clothes, with a zipper down the front that was unzipped just enough so that wisps of gray chest hair peeped out. His face was full and deeply tanned, his hair receding and almost totally white. He had powerful-looking arms and thick, beefy hands.

Standing next to Big Wyn was a thickset younger woman in a rather plain blue dress, which she kept nervously tugging at as if she were uncomfortable. Not quite chunky, she was square in her build. Her legs stuck out from the bottom of her dress like two strong fence posts and I immediately guessed she was a golfer on the tour. They have that kind of power source. Her hair was close-cropped and her face was square and deeply tanned. She was looking up at us with what seemed to be a scowl, her eyebrows thick and heavy and knitted in an unpleasant manner.

Honie and I tripped lightly down a rounded staircase to get to the lower level where everyone else was standing. Honie handled the introductions with professional aplomb. I shook hands with Big Wyn and Bergmeister, whose hand was cold from his drink.

The man in the coveralls was Harold Stilwell, Big Wyn's husband. The golfer was Julie Warren, who, it was explained to me, served on the players' council with Big Wyn. Casey smiled at me briefly from across the room, then turned and looked out the window. She seemed bored. I think I heard a soft snort from Honie, but chose to ignore it.

"Welcome, Mister Hacker," Big Wyn boomed in her deep subcontralto voice. "What can we get you to drink?"

"Scotch rocks, thanks," I said.

"Harold, get the man's drink," she ordered. "And I'll have another gin."

"Yes, dear," Harold said and made for the bar on the far side of the room.

"I'm still waiting for my white wine," Julie piped up. There was an unpleasant edge to her voice that matched her countenance. Harold stopped and looked at her. He was about to say something but caught himself and turned back toward the bar.

"Why, I believe I am about due for a refill," Bergmeister said to no one in particular and followed Harold to the bar. He lurched slightly as he rounded the glass cocktail table, and I could tell he was a drink or three ahead of the rest of us.

I noticed no one had asked Honie what she wanted, and was about to ask her myself when Big Wyn interjected.

"Thank you, Honie," she said dismissively. "If we need anything else, we'll call your room."

I saw a quick shadow of disappointment fall across Honie's face as she realized she had been asked to leave. She, too, had put some thought into her evening dress and makeup, and she looked lovely. But she quickly recovered, gave me one of her 100-watt smiles and left. I felt irritation rise. I'm not big on authority figures anyway, but I especially hate it when they step so casually on the little people of the world. But what was I going to do. Throw my drink in Big Wyn's face?

Harold came over with two drinks, mine and Big Wyn's. Julie sighed audibly. Big Wyn frowned at him. "Harold, will you please get Julie her wine?" she said imperiously. "She's waiting, you know."

"Goddamnit, Wynnona," Harold exploded. "I only got two hands, for Christ sakes. You'd think a goddam professional athlete would be able to fetch her own goddam drink. I'm not a slave, y'know."

"That'll be enough, Harold," Big Wyn thundered back. "Get her drink and get it now!"

I watched Harold's face turn a deep and dangerous shade of red. It stood in sharp contrast to his stiff white coveralls. But the man swallowed hard, turned on his heel, and headed back to the bar. I saw Julie glance after him with a haughtly look of victory.

I took a stiff belt from my glass of Scotch, and wished it was my third.

"So, Mr. Hacker," Big Wyn turned back to me, purring sweetly. "We are so glad to have you here with us this week."

"Absholutely," Benton Bergmeister agreed as he lurched back from the bar. His shin struck the edge of the same cocktail table he had earlier avoided and he stumbled slightly, spilling some of his drink onto his hand. "Damn," he muttered. He recovered, stood up straight and caught sight of a disapproving look from Big Wyn. He turned red and cast his eyes downward, then took a sip and sat down hard on the leather couch.

"I trust your room is satisfactory," Big Wyn continued pleasantly. "If you need anything special, just give Casey a call. She is in charge of making the travel and hospitality arrangements for our VIP guests, and she knows how to make these hotel people jump."

"Well," I said sweetly back, "I know *I'd* bust a gut doing whatever she wanted."

Casey turned back from staring out the window at nothing and fixed me with a totally flat, emotionless stare. Her pale blue eyes just rested on me, unseeing. Dead. Humorless. I got a bit of the willies just looking at those eyes and resisted the temptation to put a hand down between my legs to make sure everything was still there.

"And of course," Wyn continued, "Benton and I would be happy to make ourselves available for an interview at your convenience."

"Well, thanks," I replied graciously. "It's been quite a while since I last covered a women's event, and I'm looking forward to seeing some of the newer faces. Like Julie here, for instance." I nodded at the woman, who turned a little red. "How is your season going? I haven't heard much about you."

Turning redder still, Julie was about to say something when Big Wyn cut her off.

"Julie has been working closely with me on tour business this season," she said. "As a result, her golf game has suffered some. But she's been working hard in the last few weeks and we expect her game to improve shortly."

"I see," I said, and that little radar blip of irritation flared anew. I hate it when someone answers another's question like that. "So what kinds of issues have you been dealing with?" I asked Julie, looking directly at her. "Have you found some new sponsors to fill up your spring break?"

The LPGA had suffered the indignity of losing some tournament sponsors which had left a gaping hole in the early weeks of the year's schedule. So far, the tour had been unsuccessful in filling this unwanted "spring break" in their schedule.

Julie didn't even attempt to answer me this time. She just took a long, slow sip from her glass of chardonnay and looked at me over the rim of her glass with those beetled eyebrows.

Big Wyn sighed once, audibly. "I don't know why that has become such a major issue with you press people," she said with some irritation. "Instead of focusing on the thirty-eight excellent tournaments we have scheduled, you always bring up those three damn weeks when we don't have one. I'll get those weeks filled next year, so just keep your pants on."

I turned to look directly at Wyn. "Well," I said, "Since Julie apparently can't talk to me, perhaps you can point me towards a few of the newer players who are allowed to speak. Be good if you could find me a player from New England. Local angle always goes over big with my editor."

For a minute, Big Wyn stared at me. An uncomfortable silence built in the room. "Of course," she said finally, nodding to herself, eyes holding mine thoughtfully. "I'll be happy to give you a list of some of the girls you should talk to, some of the newer members of the tour. Julie, you can help Mr. Hacker with that, can't you?"

"Sure, Wyn, sure," she said, not looking to happy about the idea.

"That's very considerate of you," I said. "But I'm kinda used to going my own way on things. I like to poke around and get the lay of the place, if you know what I mean. Habits built up over the years and all that."

Big Wyn's eyes still peered into mine. I began to feel a tad uncomfortable. Like a book being read.

"I understand, Mr. Hacker," she said. "Still, I'm glad to have this opportunity to meet with you and go over some of our ground rules."

"Ground rules?" I said, trying unsuccessfully to keep the surprise out of my voice. I put my drink down on the table.

"Certainly," Big Wyn said confidentally. "Certain areas are, shall we say, not open for discussion with my girls."

I felt a sudden pounding in my ears, and glanced around quickly to see if anyone else could hear it. Harold was over by the bar, cleaning its surface with a wet rag. Bergmeister was still sitting on the couch, looking into his glass of vodka. Julie was watching me with another one of her hateful smirks. And the Delicious Dyke was still standing over by the window. But she was watching us now, and a slight smile played on her lips. She held a martini in one hand and with the other rubbed a sliver of lemon peel around and around the edge of her glass. If I hadn't known better, I'd swear she was trying to do something erotic for my benefit. But I knew better.

"Such as?" I asked quietly, waiting to hear it all before I did something about the thud-thud in my ears.

"Well," Big Wyn began. "First of all, I would like you not to dwell on the off-course earnings by our leading money winners. Everyone knows the girls can make quite a bit extra through endorsements and such, but I feel it detracts from the image of the tour as a whole. I prefer that our girls be known by what they earn on the golf course.

"Second, all figures on attendance at our tournaments will come from our marketing office. We have very scientific and accurate data that will show the true numbers on our gate receipts. Much better than the odd guesstimate.

"Third, the personal lives of our girls are off limits. We want you to write about their golf and only their golf. After all," and she smirked at me nastily, "I don't recall reading anything recently about the sex lives of the men players.

"Fourth – "

I held up my hand. I was beyond irritation now and had entered the realm of officially hot.

"Now wait just a goddam minute," I began. "In the fifteen years I've been a professional reporter, I have never, until this very minute, ever been told by anyone how I'm to go about reporting and writing my story. For you to stand there and check off your so-called ground rules as if you were reading a goddam shopping list gives you the biggest set of balls I have ever seen, male or female! I mean, have you ever heard of the First Amendment, or don't they have that in the land of the LPGA? You can take your goddam ground rules and shove them –"

"Hacker!" Big Wyn bellowed at me, jumping to her feet. "If I'm not mistaken, we have arranged for a complimentary hotel suite for you this weekend." Her cheekbones were burning red. "And for some free meals and other benefits. I think that gives us some right to –"

"That gives you the right to stick it right up your wazoo," I retorted. "Do you actually think I can be purchased for the price of a hotel room? Or a steak dinner? Jeez, Wyn, how many years have you been doing this? Where did you pick up the idea that you could just order people around like they were tin soldiers? Have you been reading a biography of Stalin or something? Nobody tells me how to write or what to write. Not even my editor, and he's an idiot."

Casey!" Big Wyn whirled on the girl in the shimmering red dress. "I want Hacker's comp cancelled immediately! If he wants to stay here, he can do it on his own nickel."

"My pleasure," Casey purred, and her dead flat eyes came alive with a taunting, sneering gleam. She gracefully put her martini glass down and slunk off.

Wynnona Stilwell turned back to me.

"I get what I pay for," she said.

I reached into my pocket and pulled out a five-dollar bill. I tossed it down on the table. "That should cover the Scotch," I said. "Plus a little extra for the waiter." I glanced over at Harold Stilwell, who was now rocking back and forth on the balls of his feet, cracking the knuckles on his meaty right hand. He stared back at me.

"I'm heading for the front desk," I said. "I'm going to get the billing put back in my name. Then, I'm going to spend the rest of my time here digging into the personal life of each and every player I meet. And I'm going to do a survey of off-course earnings. And when I file my story on Sunday, I'll be sure to mention this size of the gate. Oh, did I mention? I'm a really crappy crowd-counter."

"You little fucker," Julie Warren cried. She slammed down her wine glass and started toward me with sheer mayhem in her eyes. Big Wyn put out a hand and stopped her.

"And then I'm going to do some digging on Big Wyn and the LPGA," I said. "Hope your books are in order. I'd hate to find any financial shenanigans going on in the front office. Don't think the girls would like that, do you Wyn?"

She stared at me ominously. "Take your best shot, Hacker," she said. "Better men than you have tried and failed."

I couldn't think of anything to retort better than "so's your old man," so I just left.

FIVE

nger is a powerful human emotion. I reflected on
that, but not for fifteen minutes or so. During that
time, I was too busy seeing red. I don't remember
storming out of Big Wyn's palace, riding the private elevator
down, stomping through the lobby, pushing out the doors
and wandering aimlessly out onto the golf course. I'm damn
lucky I didn't fall into one of the Doral's lagoons and either
drown or get eaten by an alligator.

When I came back to my senses, I was holding the black
plastic knob of a ball washer in my hand. And my hand was
throbbing a little. I looked around, momentarily befuddled. I
realized I was out on the course somewhere, but in the dark,
I couldn't tell which course, or where. I had just trashed the
ball washer, snapping its top off. Off in the distance, a thou-

sand yards away, the bright lights of the hotel created a halo of light in the humid, misty air of the Miami night.

That's when I started to muse on the subject of anger. Oh, everyone gets pissed now and then. A cutting remark from the wife, a smartass crack from the kid, an insolent response an employee paid to know better. The blood pounds and the eyes narrow and sharp and ugly retorts jump unbidden to the lips.

But anger, pure and deep...that's another matter altogether. I wondered, standing out there in the dark on whatever tee, mosquitoes and other carnivorous pests zeroing in on my flesh, where the first *Homo erectus* had ever utilized the emotion as part of his survival instincts. They had hunted and killed the tiger and the mammoth out of instinct sharpened by several measures of raw fear, and driven by need and hunger. But there must have been times when the tiger had turned suddenly and dispatched the cave dweller's best friend or father or son. When the shock of that event had instaltly dispelled all sense of fear and rationality and common sense in the face of pure, blind rage. And in that overwhelming, senseless instant, the moment of pure and unadulterated rage, the snarling, fierce tiger had had no chance. No chance at all.

The tigers are gone, but the emotion remains. In these days of supposedly enlightened civilization, when the eyes go blank and red, a Saturday-night special suddenly puts an end to that bitchy-once-too-often spouse, a butcher knife is suddenly plunged into a drunken, abusive chest, or a child's arm bone is irrevocably snapped in two.

I walked slowly back to the hotel, now feeling a bit foolish. No tiger had devoured my best friend. Nothing so drastic had really happened. My professionalism had been insulted. That was all. Yet that had triggered in me that awful passion, and I had stood on the edge of the fearful abyss, peered over the side at the awful demons cavorting below, and had, for a brief moment, wanted more than anything to plunge headlong over the edge and join with them in their loathsome games.

I was in desperate need of sustenance and alcohol, a balm for the fevered soul. My feet followed the thump-thump-thump sound to the hotel's disco, a round, mirrored room with flashing lights, a long, curved bar, lots of tables around the edge set off by padded railings, and a small, parquet dance floor in the center. It was not a jam-packed night, but there were plenty of people.

I made my way to the bar and saw Honie Carlton standing in the midst of a small group of women. She was nursing a drink which looked blue in the strange lighting of the disco. As I neared, she looked up and saw me.

"Hey, Hacker!" she cried out, waving me over. "You done already? How did it go?"

"Great," I muttered. "I made myself persona non grata before the first free drink."

"Aw, c'mon. It couldn't have been that bad," she chided, grinning at me. I handed her the knob from the ball washer and saw her eyes widen in amazement. I motioned to the bartender, ordered a double Scotch on the rocks, and told her the whole story. Halfway through, she began gnawing at a knuckle, her pretty eyes wide and round and serious.

My drink arrived just as I finished my sordid tale. "Sorry," I said. "Guess I kinda got ticked off."

She blew her breath out in a rush, looking at the broken knob in her hand. Irrefutable proof of the power of my anger. Then she grinned at me and shrugged. "Aw, fuck it, Hacker," she said. "I may not have a job in the morning, but what the hell. That's tomorrow's problem. Cheers!"

She held out her glass to clink. But I was mad again.

"Goddam it," I said. "If they try to do anything to you, I'll slag her ass in every newspaper and magazine that knows how to spell the word 'golf.' That goddam, brass-balled bitch ..."

"Whoa, big fella," Honie's eyes were laughing. "I don't know what they'll do. I don't think anyone's talked back to Big Wyn for the last fifteen years. She might be upstairs having a heart attack this very second. Listen, they don't know that you and I are old friends. And they really can't fire me for bringing press people in – that's my job for Pete's sake. So forget it. C'mon, let's dance."

She grabbed my wrist and dragged me out onto the dance floor. It was suddenly crowded. As the DJ segued one record seamlessly into the next, missing nary a bass-thumping beat, the lights went down and only a rhythmic pulsing spotlight, flashing in time to the music, backlit the churning bodies on the dance floor.

Honie and I boogied. I'm no Fred Astaire, but I can keep from looking like a total dance doofus. Honie, on the other hand, had all the effortless moves of youth. She was rhythmic and fluid and sexy and carefree. Which is how it should be when you're twenty-five and alive.

The lights came up a bit when the next song started, and I could begin to see some of the other dancers surrounding us. As we whirled around, I began to recognize some of them as some of the LPGA's players. The crowd parted momentarily and I caught a glimpse of the shimmering red dress belonging to Casey Carlyle across the floor. Her back was toward me and she was dancing elegantly, but with reserved, economical movements to the jungle beat of the music. At first, I couldn't see her dance partner, only the fingertips of two hands grasping her around that lovely thin waist. Then, on cue, the couple moved slowly around and I saw Julie Warren staring at Casey with adoring eyes as they danced.

I felt a lurch, deep down inside somewhere as I watched the two women dancing, oblivious to me to anyone else. I wondered about that lurch for a moment. Homophobia? Disgust? Titillation? Combination of all of the above? I wasn't entirely sure. Like most reasonably evolved people, I knew that homosexuality exists and is an acceptable choice for consenting adults. I like to think that I am accepting and nonjudgemental. Some of my best friends, etc.

Maybe it was the openness I wasn't used to. Even those of us who profess to be open about alternative lifestyles probably prefer that they keep it to themselves, or out of public view. Perhaps a remnant of that old-fashioned idea was stirred by the sight of Julie and Casey dancing together with stars in their eyes. Or maybe it was a tiny residue of the macho that lives deep inside me, and probably most males. Casey was an attractive female person, I like attractive female persons, but she prefers dancing with other female persons…thus, an inner lurch.

As I thought these deep thoughts and continued dancing with Honie, my eyes eventually drifted back to Casey and Julie. They swing around, just a few feet from me, and I locked eyes with Casey Carlyle. She noticed me and a mean little smile played at the corners of her glossy rep lips. Her cool blue eyes held mine as with a sudden motion she pulled her stocky partner closer. The look she threw at me was clear: What you want, you can't have.

Was that it? The sexual challenge? I sighed. The battle of the sexes is ongoing and constant, but it's a fight for which I can never muster enough enthusiasm. Life is too short and too precious to waste over arguing about lines drawn in the gendered dirt.

I widened my area of vision to take in the entire dance floor, now a busy swirl. I noticed several other female couples, many of them including at least one young woman who earned her living playing tournament golf. I tried not to stare.

Honie must have known what I was looking at, because she suddenly grabbed me again and pulled me back to the bar. Going up the three steps beyond the padded railing, I stepped back to let a former U.S. Women's Open champ pass by on her way to the dance floor. She was grinning happily and holding the hand of a petite young girl with lots and lots of poufed-out strawberry blond hair.

I reclaimed my Scotch and drank most of it down. I needed it. Honie stood next to me, watching the dancing, still moving with the beat, her eyes alive.

"Wasn't that –" I nodded at the dance floor.

"Yup," she said, swinging her hips.

"And who is that she's dancing with?" I wondered.

"Her manager," she told me, with an impish smile.

"Ahhh," I said, ordering another drink.

"We're a close-knit group," Honie told me. "Lots of girls travel with their managers, business partners, caddies, teachers. Those who are married often bring their kids and husbands. The others have their significant others, or family members along."

"I didn't know Casey and Julie Warren were related," I said drily.

"Actually, I don't think they are," she said. Her face was motionless.

"I see." I watched the gyrations going on with the pulsating light and relentless beat of the music. "How do you feel about that?"

Honie shrugged. "Different strokes," she said, lifting her glass of blue something to her lips. She turned to look at me. "Happiness is a commodity that's in pretty short supply," she said. "I think you should grab onto it wherever you can find it."

"Sounds almost like you're a convert," I said, and immediately regretted it. It sounded both prying and peevish, and not at all like me. Or what I think is me.

Her eyes flared momentarily. Then she smiled. "I've got a boyfriend in Chicago," she said. "Of course, in the few months I've been working here, I have been hit on a few times."

"Really?" I said. "Does that bother you?"

She shrugged again. "Nothing I can't handle," she said. "After all, as a woman, I've been hit on ever since I reached the age of puberty."

"Well," I said, "There are workplace rules, you know. Maybe you should report it to Big Wyn as sexual harassment. Collect a few million."

"How do you know it wasn't Big Wyn who hit on me?" she asked, laughing.

That kinda shut me up. We drank our drinks and watched the dancing, me and my older-than-her-years friend.

SIX

The next morning, I ate breakfast unmolested in the hotel's coffee shop. There was no sign of a fire-breathing Wyn nor any of her minions. No sign of Honie, fired or not. Just a few dozen tourists from the north, each of whom seemed to be engaged in reading the prices from the menu out loud. "Two-fifteen for a side order of bacon, Willard! Dat's out-ray-gee-yus!"

Later, I wandered out to the practice tee to watch the women pros warming up for the day's practice round. While I don't normally cover the women's game, I had been to enough events, such as the mixed-team tournament in the fall, to know many of the players. And it had been at that event that the differences between the golfing sexes had been best illustrated for me.

"It's the muscle groups that make the biggest difference," one of the male pros had explained to me, well out of earshot of the nearest female golfer. "Women simply don't have the same kind of upper-body muscle mass that men do. In the golf swing, that means men can generate more clubhead speed. That means they can hit it further. Now these gals," and he meant women professional golfers, "They get their butts into it, and they've learned how to generate as much clubhead speed as they can. And with good rhythm and timing, they can get the clubface onto the ball. All of which adds up to distance, but they just don't have the same muscles, which is why the average male pro will always hit it longer than the average female pro."

He shook his head as we had watched some other women pros warming up on the range. "If you watch closely," he continued, "You'll see that the girls hit the ball on a lower trajectory, too. That's because without the same kind of upper-body strength, they have to use more of a sweeping motion. Men combine clubhead speed with a downward, descending blow, which is what lets them get the ball high into the air. But your average woman pro is hitting the ball shorter and on a lower trajectory. That's a damn deadly combination."

He went on to explain that while women professionals practice and play enough to overcome many of these physiological hindrances, the average woman player just has to deal with it. "Most holes, even the short par-fours, your weekend woman player is hitting driver and three-wood to just get somewhere near the green. Can you imagine playing golf, hitting three-woods into every green?" he asked.

"I'd give the game up," I had said.

"You and me both, son," the player had agreed. "Damn architects ought to give them more of a break, so they can play the same game as the men. But that would mean really shortening up many holes, and then the libbers start hollering 'whaddya mean our course is only four thousand yards? The men's course is seven thousand!' Can't win that one!" He'd shrugged and gone back to launching high hard ones from the practice tee.

I kept his theories in mind as I had watched that weekend's mixed-team event. And I had seen many examples that seemed to prove his point. I remembered one instance when the woman pro faced a shot up and over a tall tree in front of her. Once over the tree, she then had to carry the ball far enough to get over a greenside bunker. I knew a male pro would have had no trouble generating enough power and height to accomplish the task, but the woman pro eventually tried to hit a low screaming hook around the tree. The other option was denied her. She didn't have the right muscles. Too bad.

I wandered up and down the practice tee all morning, talking with some of the players, watching others swing. They were all working hard in the hot morning sun, doing the drudge work of professional golf. Honing swings, checking alignments, working on maintaining the angles, swinging in balance, developing a consistent tempo and rhythm. Those who had their swings working were cheerful and upbeat, whistling and joking as they worked. Those who were struggling were concentrating on their tasks, scowling at the ground, muttering after every swing. Some had dark circles of sweat coloring their shirts under their arms and between their breasts. This was hardly the kind of glamour most associate with the life of the touring golf professional.

For the most part, the golfers worked alone, though some had swing gurus watching, and others consulted with their caddies. They worked methodically through their bags which stood behind them like silent sentinels. The women pros had huge staff bags, like the men, although the logos of their sponsors which adorned the bags ran more to dishwasher detergents, cosmetics and soft drinks, as opposed to the men's investment firms, beer companies and automakers.

I noted another difference between the sexes: head covers. The women's bags showed that the prevailing taste in covers for their metal woods ran to pink, fuzzy things or cute, floppy-earned doggies. Your typical PGA pro would probably rather play naked than been seen with a cute, floppy-earned puppy-dog headcover.

Some of the caddies had gathered near the water keg standing at the far end of the practice range, in the shade of a spindly liveoak tree. Most of the caddies were men, although there was a sprinkling of female loopers too. Whatever the sex, the caddies still had that deeply tanned and mostly scruffy look, the universal badge of those who carry golf bags for a living. They were doing what caddies usually do: exchanging information and tips on good restaurants, can't-lose horses running at Hialeah, who had tickets to the rock concerts. Still, each kept an eye on their hard-working golfer, to see if they needed more practice balls, towels or water. Caddies are enthusiastic participants in the service economy. Or they aren't caddies for very long.

The only looper in the group that I knew fairly well was named "Bunny." I had no idea why, nor did I know what name appeared on his driver's license. But he had worked on the PGA Tour for years, for a variety of players. I approached him.

"Hey, Bunny," I said, walking up. "Who's hot?"

He nodded greetings, his smallish, deep-set eyes blinking at me.

"Bunch a kids are shootin' lights out," he told me. "Especially the ones from Asia. Hard to keep 'em straight. But for me, I'd put my cash down on the mick over there."

He nodded down the line at Patty Sheehan, one of the LPGA's established stars, who was swinging a handful of irons from her practice spot about six players away. I thanked Bunny for the information and wandered down to watch.

Normally a right-handed player, I watched as Patty flopped a wedge over upside down and began hitting balls with it left handed. Amazingly, they all went straight and true.

"You know," I called to her after watching this for a while, "They do make clubs for lefties. If you're converting, it might make it easier."

She looked over at me, laughed merrily and came over to shake hands. Patty has the right attitude about the game: Whether she's shooting sixty-eight or eighty, she's always cheerful. Upbeat, wisecracking. To her, it's only a game, and no doubt, that's why it's a game that has paid off handsomely for her.

"I do this to work on my impact skills," she told me as she went back to her left-handed drill. "Makes you focus on the clubhead coming through the hitting zone. It's also a good way to get your hand-eye coordination zeroed in."

We talked about her season to date, an injury she was getting over and a swing change she was working on. She showed me the progress: Turning around to the right side, she pulled another iron out of her bag and struck a dozen beautiful shots, all of which landed within ten feet of her target. She still had the classic, picture-perfect golf swing, full of fluid motion, perfect balance and balletic grace.

She stopped work for a moment to sip some water from a bottle in her bag. Down at the far end of the practice range, an Asian woman was hitting golf balls, surrounded by a noisy gaggle of photographers, video cameramen and a dozen other small, dark-haired, jabbering men. It was Misha Kuramoto, Japan's finest player and another perennial favorite on the LPGA Tour.

"God, how I feel for that girl," Patty mused as she stared at the crowd gathered around Misha. "They are with her always. Photographers, reporters, businessmen. Dozens of them. Every single day. She can't take a step without someone shooting her photo, jabbing a microphone in her face. It would drive me stark, raving mad."

Kuramoto was japan's Goddess of Golf. Her success on the tour had made her one of golf-crazy Japan's biggest celebrities, and made mandatory the need to chronicle her every movement and statement. She was never left alone as the gaggle of media types followed her around day after day so they could report back to the legion of fans in Tokyo exactly what the Great Misha was reading, eating and doing.

"Every time she pulls back a club, the hopes and dreams of millions of Japanese ride on it," Sheehan said. "Can you imagine that?" She shuddered and went back to her work in blissful isolation.

To those who have never played golf, and even those to whom the sport is something less than an obsession, it might be hard to image enjoying spending a couple of hours in the hot sun, watching the repetitive striking of golf balls. But I was thoroughly enjoying myself. I knew enough about the golf swing to recognize those who do it right, and on the practice tee that morning, there were several players doing it better than right. There are many who say the best way to learn a good swing is to go watch the women pros, and there is a lot of truth to that. There aren't too many idiosyncratic swings on the LPGA, and you could swear that many had been taught by Hogan himself. Certainly, one could learn a lot about timing and tempo by watching the women work. Men may hit the ball harder, but women hit it with more grace.

So I stood there and watched, interrupting some of them from time to time to talk about some esoteric point, grip changes, shoulder turns, whether or not the club should be laid off, footwork, swing thoughts. Before I knew it, it was lunchtime. And I only knew it because Honie Carlton came and told me so.

I was standing behind Betsy King, watching her smack three-woods heavenward with her easy, slow-paced, upright swing. Honie appeared at my side and grabbed my arm affectionately.

"Hey Hacker," she said, "Hungry?"

"I guess," I said. "But didn't I just have breakfast?" I glanced down at my watch. Twelve-fifteen. "Jeez," I said. "Tempus really fugited today."

Honie laughed. I like a girl who laughs at Latin jokes. Shows a certain amount of good breeding.

"Hey," I said, remembering last night. "Are you still employed around here?"

"Yeah," she grinned. "I got called on the carpet, though. You are definitely on their shit list. From now on, any media I want to invite has to be approved by the commissioner and Big Wyn. They patted me on the head and said all young people make mistakes. I almost puked."

"I woulda told 'em to go sit on a six-iron," I said hotly.

"Yeah, well, you're you and I'm not," she said. "And I still have plans for the future here, I guess."

"I suppose," I said. "I guess I just have a lower puke threshold than you."

"On that pleasant note, let's go get something to eat," Honie said and we began walking back to the hotel. "You know, you've become something of a celebrity with the girls," she peeked at me mischievously.

"Oh, crap, have they been peeking at me in the shower again?" I said. "Happens all the time."

Honie laughed. I liked her laugh: merry and natural. There was not much pretense in this one. "The word got around," she said, "That you told Big Wyn off last night. Something about having big balls for a woman?"

"I oughta wash your mouth out with soap," I said sternly. "Besides, why would that make me a hero? I thought everyone around here thinks Big Wyn hung the moon and the stars."

"Oh, not everybody," Honie assured me. "There is a certain vocal faction which obeys her every command, but most of the players, while they respect her achievements in the game, get a little tired of her imperious ways. I would say that if there was a popularity contest, Big Wyn probably wouldn't come in first." She paused. "Assuming it was a secret ballot, of course."

We made for the Grill Room, which had windows overlooking the famous 18th hole of the Blue Monster. There was a fountain sprouting a tall geyser from the lake that guarded the left side of that famed hole. The restaurant set up a long and groaning buffet table along the inside wall, and the tables were grouped near the window for diners to enjoy the view.

Benton Bergmeister swooped down on us like a hungry buzzard as soon as we entered the room. He must have been watching for us. Today he was waring an impeccable double-breasted blue blazer with nicely pressed seersucker trousers. Instead of a necktie, he wore a rakish scarf decorated in a garish paisley design of bright blues and reds. He was shod in black-and-white patent loafers with accents of shiny brass. It was all so very dapper. He also carried a low, wide glass containing something clear and on the rocks, with a military-tint olive floating happily among the ice cubes.

"Hacker, dear boy," he gushed. "And Miss Carlton. You must come and have lunch with me."

"I dunno," I said. "I'm not in any personal danger, am I? You aren't planning to stab me repeatedly with your cocktail sword, are you?"

"Ah ha ha ha," he gushed. "Not at all, not at all. I think we need to start over. Got off a bit on the wrong foot last night. Please, help yourself to some lunch and come join me...my table's over there." He motioned to a banquette in the corner. "I'll just go get another little libation." He set off one way and we went through the line.

"'Stab me with your cocktail sword?'" Honie giggled as we loaded up our plates.

"Okay, so I flunked rejoinder 101," I said. "It's the best I can do without some preparation time."

"I thought it was pretty good," she told me.

There was a small plate in front of Bergmeister when we sat down, nothing but a few bread crumbs on it. He had apparently decided to lunch liquidly today. As we sat down, he was washing down a handful of pills with his drink.

"Hope those are all legal," I chided. "Wouldn't be good press if the public learned the LPGA commish was a secret druggie."

He laughed again and shook his head. "Not at all, Mister Hacker," he said. "When you get to be my age, things begin to wear out and drop off. It can be quite alarming. The medical profession, bless their evil hearts, stands ready to prescribe an entire pharmacopoeia to cure all my aches and pains. One for the heart, one for the blood pressure, two for this, three for that." He sighed. "It's hell getting old."

He started to put his pill bottle back in his pocket, then shook it and said to no one in particular. "I meant to have this refilled before I left home. Didn't think I'd run out so soon."

"Call Casey," Honie suggested. "She can get it refilled for you at a local drugstore."

I took a moment to study Benton's face as he and Honie chatted idly about tour business. The bushy gray hair was carefully combed back behind his ears. In fact, everything about the man was careful and precise: his clothes, his hair, his bearing. But I could see the artificial shades of red across his brow and cheeks; the ever-so-slightly visible capillaries; the darkened hoods above the eyes. My years of hanging around with Boston cops, those loveable, Irish, two-fisted drinkers of boilermakers – shots of Bushmills washed down with a foamy beer – had enabled me to study the faces of some truly prodigious drinkers. I knew the telltales, and I saw them even on the carefully presented face of Benton Bergmeister.

He eventually turned to me and leveled his gray-green eyes at me earnestly.

"I feel I really must apologize for the unpleasantness of last evening," he murmured. "Mrs. Stilwell has been under a great deal of pressure recently. She still maintains a busy schedule of tournament play because the fans still want to watch her play. At the same time, her duties as president of the tour council require a great deal of administrative energy. I really believe she was just tired last night."

"Well, it's very nice of you to try and explain away her behavior," I said. "But she acted like a horse's ass. If she wants to tell me she's sorry herself, I can probably find it in my heart to forgive her. Everyone's allowed at least one mistake."

He took a long pull on his drink.

"Quite," he said finally. "May I then tell Wyn that the hatchet is officially buried and that we may expect a favorable article?"

I stared at him a minute, then turned and looked at Honie. She paused in midbite when she saw the look on my face. "'Scuse me," she said hurriedly, "I just remembered a call I have to make." She fled.

Bergmeister's question still hung in the air. He was idly stirring the ice cubes in his glass with one finger. He cocked his head at me as if he had just asked me if I would like one lump or two in my tea.

"You people are unreal," I said slowly. "You never give up, do you?"

He colored. I'll give him that much. He had enough decency to be a little embarrassed.

"Well—" he began.

"No," I interrupted. "You listen to me, Benton. I want you to understand my position here. I am a professional journalist. People do not tell me what to write or how to do my job, unless they are the ones handing me a paycheck. If I happen to write something you judge to be unpleasant, or unfair, or that you just don't like, that's tough. You can write a letter to the editor and complain about me. If I happen to write something you judge to be libelous, you can sue me. And good goddam luck on that.

"Now, I was planning to do some kind of overview piece here this weekend, something more than just a game story on who wins the tournament and how. Women's golf is booming in popularity and theoretically, the LPGA should be in the vanguard of that popular wave. But I've found something more interesting here. You and I both know that the tour is struggling, having trouble attracting sponsors and finding places to play tournaments. You're losing dollars to the PGA Tour and even to their senior circuit.

"Now why is that? I'm beginning to get a picture of a business organization that is run by a pushy bitch who seems to take as her organizational model some South American tinhorn dictatorship. It doesn't seem to be working. And as for you, I see a commissioner who's not only her powerless front man and apologist, but a semi-alcoholic to boot."

I paused. Benton's face had gone white.

"Now that's a hell of a story. My readers would like to know more about that. So I plan to do a little more digging. Talk to some players. Maybe some of the tour's sponsors. Get some people on the record. How's that sound? I think it's gonna make a nice little piece. How 'bout another pop? I'll buy."

I got up and left Benton sitting there, face turning alternately red and white, his shoulders suddenly slumped. On the way out, I passed a table at which the lovely Julie Warren was staring at me, her formidable eyebrows beetling at me furiously. My mood was suddenly sour enough to join the battle, so I walked over to her.

"Hello, Julie my love," I said sweetly. "Strangled any beagles with your bare hands today? Leapt any buildings in a single bound? How 'bout castrated any sportswriters? I hear that's a big favorite with you."

She rose slowly out of her chair so that, standing, she was closer to being eyeball-to-eyeball.

"You're a lousy, good-for-nothing fucker," she said in a low menacing voice. "And I'm telling you, you better watch your goddam back." She was jabbing her forefinger at my chin.

I grabbed her hand, forefinger and all, and, raising it to my lips, planted a noisy, European-style kiss on it. People at the nearby tables were watching.

"God, I love it when you talk tough, dear," I said. "It gives me tingles all over."

As I walked away, I was thinking to myself "My rejoinders are getting better all the time."

SEVEN

That afternoon, I decided to trail around the golf course after Mary Beth Burke. She was playing a practice round with a younger player I didn't know. "Burkey" was a favorite of mine. And a few million other fans. She came onto the LPGA scene a few years after Big Wyn had established her domination, Where Big Wyn played a stunning power game. Mary Beth had won our hearts for her pluckiness. Back in the day, she had reminded us of that mythical girl next door: small, tousled-haired, freckle-faced. She played the game with a ready, toothy grin and a never-say-die attitude.

There had been a handful of monumental, last-day battles between Mary Beth Burke and Big Wyn. Big Wyn slashing her furious drives and pounding long irons into tight pins. Mary Beth hanging tough, keeping her ball in play, draining those exciting no-brainers -- long putts that no one expects to make. It had been legend-making golf on the order of Palmer vs. Nicklaus or Hogan vs. Snead, mainly because neither rival was viewed by the public as the bad guy. Big Wyn's style was power and dominance and was hugely admired by her fans. Burkey was all heart. With her happy grin and tousled hair combined with that inner determination to keep, by God, trying...well, you couldn't ever root against her, either.

While Mary Beth was a few years younger than Big Wyn, her best golf, too, was probably behind her. She still played a fairly active tournament schedule, but I knew she was also spending more and more time teaching younger girls. I imagined she'd be good at teaching: never critical in a harsh way, always stressing the positive and always planting the seeds of her indomitable desire to do better.

Her hair was still tousled, but it had gone a bit gray in places. Her grin was still there and so were the freckles. I had interviewed Mary Beth the first time when she had won the U.S. Women's Open and ran into her from time to time over the years.

I strolled out to the first tee where she and her playing partner were loosening up, waiting for the group ahead to clear the fairway. There weren't many fans out to watch the practice rounds, so I walked right up and caught Mary Beth's eye.

"Hacker!" she cried and came running over to the ropes, that incandescent grin lighting up her famous face. "Oh, it's good to see you again! I heard that you were down here this week. What's it been. Two years?"

I kissed her on the cheek and returned her hug. "At least that much," I said. "They don't let me out much anymore. Mind if I tag along for a few holes?"

"That's be super!" she said. "As long as you promise not to write anything about my bad shots. There are too many of them these days." She waved to the other golfer to come over. "Carol, c'mere. This is Pete Hacker from Boston. He's a golf writer and a damn good one, too. Hacker, meet Carol Acorn. She's been working with me lately."

"Then she must be a damn good one, too," I said. Carol and I shook hands. She was a rangy blond whose straight hair was pulled back in a pony tail and tucked behind her golf visor. She had the broad shoulders and long, tanned arms of a golfer. Her crisp white golf shorts emphasized her powerful legs. Her eyes were a clear, no-nonsense blue.

"C'mon, Carol, hon," Burkey piped. "Let's whack 'em."

Mary Beth drove first, coiling her short but powerful form slowly, then releasing into the ball with a furious motion that sent the clubhead rocketing into the ball. To the sound of a resounding *whack*, her tee shot took off down the fairway straight and true. The other few fans and I applauded and were rewarded with the patented Mary Beth Burke grin and a soft wave of thanks.

Carol Acorn then took the tee. She stood behind her ball and focused those clear blue eyes at her target before stepping up to the ball. Once settled in over the ball, she paused again for several long moments, waggling once or twice and turning her head to look down the fairway twice. Her swing, as it unfolded slowly before me, looked technically correct, but I noted a few subtle twitches and a discernable stiffness in the motion. It did not look natural to me like Burkey's time-honed swing. It was the golf swing of a robot, not a dancer. Programmed by computer, not inspired by the Muse. Uptight, not relaxed. Still, the result was fine, a long, high-arching drive down the middle. We applauded for her, too.

Mary Beth motioned for me to come inside the ropes and walk with her. Since it was practice and no one was around anyway, there was no problem. Between shots, we caught up on old times. Burkey told me she'd been divorced for a few years, but comfortably so. "Hell, poor old Benny was in a lose-lose situation," she told me. "If he stayed back home in Texas, people would talk about him lettin' his woman roam the world without her man. If he came out on tour with me, he became Mr. Mary Beth Burke. He spent a couple of years bein' miserable until I finally told him it was time to do something else. It was like letting a man out of jail, Hacker," she laughed. "We're still the best of friends, now that the pressure's off, and when I'm home in Odessa, we spend a lot of time together. Maybe in a couple more years, when I retire for good, we can try again. He's a damn good man."

"And you're a hell of a woman," I told her. She rewarded me with another hug.

Maybe it was just the pressure-free environment of a Tuesday practice round, nothing on the line, few fans around. Maybe it was the attention she was giving to her student as they played. Maybe it was the fun she was having talking to me about golf and golfers we both knew. Whatever, I certainly didn't see any erosion in her golf skills that afternoon. Without even trying hard, she was playing a brilliant round.

Never one with great length off the tee, she kept her ball in the fairway. Then she rifled crisp iron shots right at the pins. On the few occasions when she missed a green, her short game was flawless, getting her up and down out of bunkers and rough with ease. And her putting stroke seemed tuned in. Burkey was a player.

On the tenth fairway, we stood together and watched Carol Acorn prepare her seven-iron approach to a well-guarded green. Again, there was the deliberate pre-planning followed by the robotic swing. Again, the results were satisfactory, if not spectacular. Carol's shot hit the green, but a good twenty-five feet from the pin.

"There's a touch of stiffness in that swing," I commented as we walked out of Carol's earshot up to the green.

"Absolutely A-One correct, Hacker," Mary Beth nodded. "The girl is a golfer. Knew that the minute I laid eyes on her. But I'm having a god-awful time trying to get her to let go and just swing the club. You've noticed that she hasn't said one word to either of us yet. She's wound up way too tight."

It was true. Mary Beth and I had been chatting and joking between shots, carrying on a nonstop conversation. But Carol Acorn had kept to herself, speaking only briefly to her caddie and otherwise concentrating only on her golf game. Her eyes remained hidden in the shadows of her visor.

Burke laughed. "Once, on the practice tee, I asked her what she was thinking before and during her swing. Y'know, we all usually have some kind of swing thought. Like 'Smooth it,' or "Slow back,' or something like that?"

I murmured agreement.

"Well, this girl starts rattling off all the things she was trying to think about while she swung her golf club. I mean, she was telling herself not to cup her left wrist and to maintain the proper angles with her arms and to feel the clubface open going back and moving her left knee three inches to the right. My God!" Burke shook her head and laughed. "After fifteen minutes of this crap I almost took my driver out and smacked her with it! Good God Almighty...this game is hard enough without cluttering up your head with all that other shit!"

I laughed. "What was it that Bobby Jones used to say? If he was thinking about two things before every swing, he might shoot par. If he only had one swing thought going, he said he felt he always had a chance to win the tournament."

"Damn right," Burkey said. We reached the green. Carol's ball was away. She began stalking her putt. First she crouched behind it for a long minute. Then she began walking in a 360-degree circle around the hole, studying the angles, the break, the grain. Then, back at the ball, she took about six practice strokes.

I heard Mary Beth audibly sigh. "Hey Carol," she called out. We both looked over at her. Mary Beth cocked her head over, cirled her fingers next to her ear as if she was grasping an imaginary drain plug and pulled, making a loud popping noise as she did. She held the drain plug open for a while, cocking her eyebrows at her student.

Carol Acorn and I both laughed, and understood the pantomime. Empty your head,' she was saying. This is only a practice round. Stop thinking and just do.

Carol backed away from her putt for a moment and then, still smiling, laid her putter behind the ball, took one brief peek at the hole and stroked the putt. It rolled, with that uncanny inerrant accuracy that well-struck putts always have, right into the heart of the hole. Mary Beth shouted "yeah!" and pumped the air with her fist. Carol laughed.

She also loosened up immeasurably after that and began to sharpen up her game. Her swing smoothed out and her shots began to land around the pins as if guided by radar. She even began to walk with an extra spring in her step, buoyant and confident. Mary Beth watched her student relax and play better and glowed with pride.

It was on the sixteenth hole that I accidently crossed her wires. The sixteenth on the White is a medium-length par-three over a large pond that fronts the green. The green is slightly raised and fronted by a low stone wall that rises out of the water. Deep bunkers cut into both sides, but in the back of the green, and down the entire left side along the pond's edge, the greenskeeper had planted beds of flowers. The riot of colors softened the effect of the hole, reflecting off the still water of the black pond. But it was still a difficult shot to that narrow green, requiring about a five-iron.

Carol had just made a lovely birdie on the par-five fifteenth and I walked with her though a pine glade on the way to the sixteenth tee.

"Your game is looking better by the hole," I said to her.

"Thanks, Mr. Hacker," she said, a happy lilt to her voice. "Mary Beth is a wonderful teacher. When she can get me to relax, I always play much better."

"How do you like the life of a professional?"

She blew out her breath in a whoosh. "It's been quite an experience," she said, shaking her head. "I thought college golf was tough, but this is an entirely different level. I've played in eight tournaments so far this year and thought I was playing pretty well. Missed the cut in four and my best finish is a tie for eighteenth! But the other girls have been real nice…encouraging, y'know? I've had a good time and I think I'm getting better every week."

"Have you ever played a round with Big Wyn Stilwell?" I asked.

She reacted to my question as if I had slapped her full across the face. She stopped in her tracks and stared at me, her face drained of color. Her eyes went suddenly dark and cold.

"Wh-what did you say?" she asked, her tone dead. "Wh'what do you mean by that?"

Mary Beth, who had been trailing us by a few steps, came up and we both stared in amazement at the look in the girl's eyes.

"I mean, have you played with Big Wyn yet in a tournament?" I said, more than a little perplexed. "Has she seen your swing yet?"

"No," Carol snapped and abruptly walked on. Mary Beth cocked an eye at me in silent wonder and hurried to catch up with her protégé. To give them a moment, I wandered over to a water cooler and filled a paper cup.

Thanks to her birdie on the last hole, Carol teed off first. I could tell she was still upset about something. Her preshot routine was forgotten. She grabbed a club from her bag, teed her ball and took a quick, hurried swipe of a practice swing. Her quick, angry jab dug up a hefty divot. She took two more practice swings. Two more thick divots flew through the air.

"Hey honey," Mary Beth cracked. "Leave a little turf for the rest of us."

Carol didn't respond. She looked at the hole, stepped up to her ball and swung. Along with her composure, Carol Acorn had also lost her golf swing. Her backswing was hurried and off plane. She never paused at the top, but rushed her downswing and tried to compensate for an incomplete backswing with a pulling move. On top of that, her hips were all out of rhythm with the rest of her body, and she ducked her head downwards at the last moment.

It was an ugly, ugly swing with an ugly, ugly result. The clubhead got hooded, moving from outside-in, and it jammed heavily into the turf. The ball flew sickly to the right at about a forty-five degree angle, carried at most about fifty yards and dropped into the pond with a sickening plop. It was the worst shank-swing of a twenty-eight handicapper, a twice-a-monther. It was the sort of golf shot that occurs almost daily at country clubs and municipal courses across the land, and almost never at a professional event. It was shocking.

There were maybe six people standing there watching. I heard one universal, sharp intake of breath. The two caddies stared at their feet. I didn't know what to say. Mary Beth stared at her young student, unbelieving. I know she wanted to say something funny to break the tension, but she seemed to understand that humor wouldn't work right here, right now. She was shocked into silence.

Carol held the pose of her finish and watched the ripples spread slowly out from the entry point of her ball. Those terrible, ever-widening circles that were indelible proof of a diasterously bad shot. Then, she slowly lowered her club, walked silently over to a bench at the side of the tee, sank down heavily on it, buried her face in her hands and began, silently, to weep. Her broad shoulders shook.

Mary Beth hurried over, knelt down, and began to comfort the girl in soft, whispered tones. Carol seemed unconsolable. She couldn't talk as wave after wave of some deeply buried sadness came bursting forth. That it was all so silent was even worse.

I was stunned. And I felt terrible. Obviously, something I had said had triggered this. I followed Mary Beth to the girl's side.

"Carol," I began, "If I said something that upset you, I'm really sorry."

Her head came up out of her hands for just a moment. I saw the red, angry splotches on her face. And I saw into her eyes. In that brief moment, I saw an unspeakable torment. Eyes from the Inferno. Eyes that revealed a terrible anguish and begged for relief from her private hell. But it was just for an instant, because she buried her head in her arms again, turning away in misery, another wave of silent, shoulder-shaking sobs overtaking her.

Mary Beth, who seemed as perplexed as I, waved me away. There was nothing I could do. "I'll catch up with you later," I told Mary Beth and turned away.

I felt awful as I trudged back to the clubhouse. I wondered what it had been that set the girl off so dramatically. Had the ugly brutality of that one bad shot been enough to send her over the edge? Did she take the game that seriously? Had our small talk upset her in some way. What had we been talking about?

Big Wyn. I had mentioned the name and she had received a psychic jolt. Big Wyn Stilwell. There must be something there, hanging between the two. Big Wyn and Carol. Something that would cause the gates of hell to open for the younger girl and let whatever demons she had inside come dancing out with the red-hot pitchforks and fiendish cackles and burning hot eyes and chase that girl's mind down and down into a region of boiling cauldrons and steaming, unrelenting heat.

EIGHT

Mary Beth Burke came looking for me later that night and found me in one of the hotel's bars. I was deep in conversation with a dentist from Pittsburgh. It was an intellectual discussion involving batting averages, earned-run averages, and slugging percentages of various members of our respective ballclubs. Inasmuch as I'm a golf writer and was deep into about my fourth Scotch of the night, I was proud of myself for holding my own in the conversation, even though I was making things up with both sides of my brain. I was, of course, defending the honor of my beloved Sox, while the dentist seemed strangely attached in a similar way to his "'irates." From the looks we were starting to get from our fellow imbibers, we might have been getting just a tad too loud.

When Mary Beth saw me, she came over, took one look at me and then pulled me off my barstool. "C'mon," she said, "Let's take a walk."

April in Florida is a pleasant time, about the last pleasant time until the end of November. The days are balmy without being overbearing or humid and at night the breeze drifts in off the water and brings with it a hint of a cleansing chill. The worst of the blood-sucking summer bugs have yet to appear. I've always figured the most carnivorous bugs go south to Cuba for the winter and fly back across the Straits of Florida in time to enjoy the summer furnace of heat and humidity after having been made especially angry by a few months of life under Fidel's regime. In another few weeks, say by the middle of May, the air will turn into a solid wall of humidity. Then, all the breeze does is move the wall around slowly and ponderously, forcing it up under your clothing to dark bodily places that begin to prickle and itch.

But as we strolled aimlessly through the softly lit hotel grounds, that whispering breeze was as caressing and refreshing as a sip of cold blush wine. It took the buzz out of my head. Mary Beth did the rest.

At first she did a lot of fidgeting and sighing and mumbling to herself as we walked. I let it sit for a time while I enjoyed the night air. On the fourth sigh, I finally turned to her.

"Okay, Burkey," I said sternly. "Out with it. What kind of burr is under your saddle?"

"I need to talk with you – with someone—about Carol," she said. "But…I'm not so sure you're the one. You being press and all." She wouldn't look me in the eye.

"Look, Mary Beth," I said, "I've got enough to write about without laying open some poor girl's personal problems. My readers really don't give a crap about that stuff. They want to know who won and why. Now I don't know what set her off out there today, and I guess you're fixing to tell me. If it's something really dark and deep, don't tell me. Go find a priest or a shrink or something. But if you think I could help with something, I'll listen. And I don't have to tell you, of all people, that it'll be off the record if that's what you want."

She smiled at me finally. "Thanks, Hacker," she said. "You'll do just fine."

We found a bench and sat down. In the relative quiet of the evening, the incessant sounds of the city invaded the walls of our lush refuge. A siren wailed off in the distance, and a steady thunder built in intensity as a jet from the nearby airport roared its way down the runway.

"I didn't know what the hell happened to Carol out there today," Burkey began. "It scared the everlovin' crap out of me to tell you the truth. She's such a steady, serious girl. Works real hard at her game and she's totally dedicated to getting better. Hell, if anything, I'd say she works too hard at it. But you know me...I'm from the 'let 'er fly and have some fun' school anyway. But she's always been so level-headed, I've never seen any emotion from her at all, on or off the golf course. I thought she was cracking up. I got her off the golf course and holed up in the locker room. Took me a couple hours before I could make any sense out of her."

"I mentioned Big Wyn Stilwell to her," I said. "That seemed to be the trigger. Don't know why."

"Well, you're close enough to the dance floor to hear the music," Burkey said. "Do you remember what it was you said?"

"I just asked her if Big Wyn had ever seen her swing," I said, thinking back.

"No, you asked her if she'd ever played a round with Big Wyn," Burkey said quietly.

"OK," I nodded. "So…?"

She didn't say anything. I thought for a minute.

"Wait a minute," I exclaimed, turning to look at Mary Beth. "Played a round. Played around. You mean to tell me she thought I was asking if she'd ever …"

Burke exhaled and nodded. I was speechless. "I know, I know," she said. "It sounds like a line from about a dozen bad jokes that you and I both know. But there's a bit more to it. And this is where it gets ugly, Hacker."

She paused and looked out into the night. She chewed on her lower lip and clasped and unclasped her hands.

"Look, Hacker," she said finally. "You're a growed-up man and you've been around. I guess it's no big news to you that there are some girls out here who like to fool around with other girls."

"Yeah, well, that's fairly common knowledge," I said. "Despite all the official tap dancing about the subject, everyone seems to understand that a group of professional women athletes tends to include a higher percentage of homosexuals than the general population. So what? Aren't we past all that?"

"Well, yes and no," Mary Beth said slowly. "I think most folks believe that what you do at night under the sheets and with whom is pretty much your own private business. And from what I understand, that way of life has existed on the Tour since there has been a Tour. It's only lately that some of the girls are becoming more comfortable with more overt expressions of their sexuality. But most still keep that part of their lives hidden from the rest of the world. The girls out here may be having sex every which way, but most of them don't talk about it or flaunt it in public. It's still kind of taboo."

She paused again, thinking.

"You gotta understand something, Hacker," she said. "The PR people and the Tour like to tell folks that we're all one big happy family out here on the LPGA Tour. I don't think that's quite accurate. We're really more of a ... a small town, if you think about it. I should know—I'm a small-town girl myself. I mean, there are about 150 players, and our caddies, and our friends and families and business managers and whoever. Amd we're all kinda bound up together in what we do. When you think about it, that's pretty close to what a small town is. Except in our case, instead of being all together in one place, like Podunk, Iowa, we all travel around from place to place every week."

"A moveable Peyton Place," I said, suddenly understanding. "Same people, same life, different locale every week."

"Right," Burkey said, nodding at me approvingly. "And like any small town, everybody knows everyone else's business, and then some. I get a wart on my butt, everybody knows all about it inside a day. Then they all come over with butt-wart remedies!"

I had to laugh. "So what you're telling me is that Carol slept with Big Wyn and everyone knew it? So why did she freak out?"

"No, that's not it at all," Burkey corrected me, "Nobody knew nothing. Look, I told you high tightly wound Carol is. She's got this one-track mind: golf, golf, and golf. I don't know what that girl does for fun, but I can just about guarantee that sex isn't on the agenda."

She paused again, her lips pursed.

"You see, we all pretty much know who does what and with whom," she said. "When a girl first comes on tour, it's part of the list. She plays Taylor Made woods, Titleist ProV1 balls, and sleeps with girls or doesn't. And that last part is about as important as the first two: It's just a part of who you are. I don't know anyone who's terribly judgmental. We all just try to get along and play some golf and make some money."

She turned to look at me.

"What I'm saying is that even though we all know what's going on, we don't much care. But the word on Carol was that she was one of the nonsex girls."

"Nonsex?" I asked.

"Someone who doesn't really care about sex," she said. "Someone so into their golf game that they just don't do it. Period. Too busy practicing and playing and all. Carol Acorn is one of them."

She looked off at the lights twinkling in the distance and we listened to the breeze rustling the palm fronds above us.

"When I'm working with a girl, I always try to get to know her personally a bit," she continued. "You know, go out and have a few beers. Do some girl talk. I like to find out what makes 'em tick. Hell, people think professional golfers are magic somehow. We're just folks like anyone else. Anyway, this girl never opened up with me. Hell, I had to practically tie her up and drag her out the door to get her to out with me sometimes. Always had her guard up, never let anyone inside. The original and still champeen Ice Maiden."

She shook her head sadly. "Just no fun in that girl, It's so sad. But I see it all the time. These girls coming up are just so determined to win, no matter the cost. It gets their life outta whack, if you know what I mean. If you spend your entire life chasing the rainbow and never get it, leaves you kinda empty inside."

"And Big Wyn?" I asked.

Mary Beth pursed her lips before answering.

"Wynona Stilwell is one of the best golfers who every played the game," she said carefully. "But she is not a nice person. She has never let anything or anybody stand in the way of getting whatever it is she wants. And she wants it all."

"Such as…" I prompted.

"Well, hell it's no secret that Wyn runs this show," Mary Beth said. "You know, all that woman has ever done in her life is play golf. She made it to the top and stayed there a long time."

"And now?"

"And now her ability as a player has lessened. Hell, age does that to everybody. And we don't have a Woman's Senior Tour…yet!"

We both laughed.

"I think she got into the administrative side of the game as a way to keep control, keep her hand it," Burkey said. "She decided if she could no long play her way to the top, she'd just take over and run the joint. She likes being the top dog."

"But the general impression is that she's done a pretty good job," I said.

"Oh, hell, she's done a great job," Burke said. "Purses are up, sponsors are happy, we're getting a bit more television coverage every year. But ..." She trailed off.

"I remember there was some locker-room talk a few years ago when she was elected president of the players' council about some people she stepped on hard. And there are still whispers about how she manages to pull off some of her deals. Heck, we're all self-employed and independent minded, so when an issue comes up, everyone has an opinion. Somebody who disagrees with Big Wyn gets called into a meeting to discuss it, and comes out saying 'I was wrong, this'll be great!' But you look at them casting their eyes sideways at Big Wyn and you wonder what was said in that room. Now, I'm beginning to understand a little." She blew out a frustrated and angry breath.

"Carol told me what happened, finally. It was about a year ago. Carol was new on Tour and struggling. Wyn came up to her one day and offered to work with her on her game. 'Wow,' she thought, 'Big Wyn Stillwell wants to help me!'

"So they go spend an afternoon on the practice tee. Then Big Wyn invites her back to the room to watch some swing videos. Wine gets poured. Girls just havin' fun. Two or three wines. Probably something in them. Carol wakes up in Wyn's bedroom. Wyn is doing some things to her she just doesn't understand."

Mary Beth's voice began to shake.

"Carol is horrified. She jumps up and starts to leave. Big Wyn laughs and pushes her down and starts in on the hard sell. Tells her that to win on the LPGA, a girl's gotta pay her dues. Gotta concentrate on golf, not men. Men are messes and trouble and there's no room for them. Tells her the good players have always known this, and that's why they stick to the girls-only in the sex department. Uncomplicates things, she says. Simplify the sex life and let the golf roll."

"What a crock," I said.

"Yeah, well, like I said, it was the hard sell," Burkey said. "And when Carol still balked, Big Wyn dropped the other shoe. Told her their little party had all been captured on videotape. And Carol's got two choices. She can come back for more and welcome to it. Or she can just bide her time until Big Wyn needs a favor and then decide what's more important to her: Doin' Big Wyn's favor or having her sex life exposed in all the tabloids. First one to get the tape would be Carol's daddy."

"Christ," I said, awed by the evil of it all.

"Yeah," Burkey agreed. "And poor ole Carol, the champeen Ice Maiden, locks all this up inside. All the memories and the guilt and the bad feelings and the humiliation, and keeps it there for about a year."

"Until Hacker the scribe asks her a simple and innocent question," I finished.

Burke nodded sadly. "Whereupon it all came out like a gusher."

"What are you going to do?" I asked.

"I sent Carol home," Mary Beth said. "Withdrew her from the tournament. Contacted her family, packed her on the next plane. Called her brother and said the girl probably could use some counseling and some time away from golf."

We sat in silence for a long time, each locked into our own thoughts. It's always sobering to encounter the evil that lurks in the human soul. It hides in there within all of us, and most of us spend our waking hours trying hard to keep that particular demon locked safely away.

But then there are those who revel in it. Who let their personal evils come out and play every day. Who enjoy the power and the rush and obliterating laugh of the daily fix. Who go through life happily destroying and tearing down and burning bridges.

It's no fair fight between Good and Evil. None of us have the purity of heart and soul to effectively battle those who let their evil impulses rule their lives. We're all just trying to hang on, do the best we can, and carve a little happiness out of this large mess of a world. And then come the Evil Ones, catching us unaware from behind. Scything and slaying blindly, cutting down all in their path for the nasty joy of it. As we fall, with our last conscious thoughts, we can hear their victorious cackles echo in our minds.

NINE

It was Wednesday morning when the telephone woke me. Early Wednesday morning. Too damn early. I had planned to sleep in. It was, after all, supposed to be my vacation and I needed to catch up on my sleep. Especially since I had returned to the hotel bar after hearing Mary Beth's sordid tale and gotten myself rip-roaring drunk. But it was a little after eight when the telephone woke me. I checked the time on my bedside clock radio, groaned, closed my eyes and fumbled the phone to my ear.

"Morning, Hacker!" chirruped Honie Carlton's obscenely cheerful voice. "Up and at 'em, big guy. A new day dawns."

"Ah, for cryin' out loud," I moaned. "Can't you just leave me alone until lunch? I promise I'll write nothing but superlatives about the goddam Tour…just let me sleep!"

My head was pounding. My tongue felt thick and fuzzy. In general, I felt like crap.

"I got a better idea," Honie said. "How about an entire whole day at the beach? Doing nothing but catching some rays, drinking pina coladas and watching the parade of beach bunnies. South Beach, Hacker. I hear they don't wear bathing suit tops over there."

I opened one eye. "You are, as they say, playing my song," I told Honie. "What's the catch?"

"Hacker, you are so cynical," Honie pouted. "What makes you think there's a catch?"

"Honie, there is always a catch," I said. "Always."

"Well, today is just a practice round. Tomorrow's the pro-am. But there is a little Chamber of Commerce thingy over at the Fountainbleu at noon," she told me.

I moaned and reclosed my eye. My head began throbbing in a higher key.

"But," she quickly finished. "You don't have to do anything. I just promised I'd have you there. As far as I'm concerned, you can park it on a chaise and wave and that'll count as an appearance. After all, I can't make you work, can I?"

I laughed appreciatively. "Okay, you win," I surrendered. "When and where?"

I'll come get you in an hour," she giggled. "Bring your sun block."

I ordered lots of coffee and breakfast from room service, had a quick shower, downed a few aspirin and perused the morning newspaper that had been laid outside my door. The local sportswriters were waxing ecstatic about the world's best women players about to play in their town. Someone had done an interview piece with Big Wyn A sidebar listing all her tour victories covered almost an entire column. The front of the sports section had a big four-color photo of Stilwell. They had taken two pictures: one in golf clothing, holding her driver; one in business attire, clasping a brief-case. The two photos had been PhotoShoped into one, to illustrate the two roles of Big Wyn.

The story was effusive in its praise of Big Wyn and the job she had been doing for the Tour. It mentioned the spon-sors she had personally corralled, the tournaments she had helped arrange and the many, many personal appearances she made. It made her sound like a selfless giver, instead of a vicious, power-hungry, manipulative bitch.

By the time Honie appeared to collect me, I had downed most of the pot of coffee and was feeling semi-human again. Honie was wearing khaki shorts with a white top that cov-ered her bathing suit. She also carried a big straw hat and sunglasses.

"Planning on working hard today, huh?" I jested.

"Well, hell, I deserve it, the hours I've been putting in," she said. "Besides, my only assignment for the day is to en-tertain you. So prepare to be entertained, as long as its on the beach."

Carl packed us into a taxi and we set off across the various causeways to Miami Beach. Sun-and-fun capital of the world. Jackie Gleason and the June Taylor Dancers. Yachts bobbing in marina after marina, and high-rises glistening above the azure sea, home to a new generation of glitterati. Of course, one had to speak Spanish in order to communi-cate with anyone, except in South Beach, where all you needed was hard abs, roller-blades and the ability to grunt in single syllables.

The reality? Block after block of numbingly depressing motel units, all housing elderly people engaged in a race against time. Which would run out first...the money or life? Days spent waking up, sipping prune juice, popping the colorful array of pills, wandering down to the corner to sit outside, try to make the newspaper last the morning, studying the obits for the names of friends. When the money got tight, cutting back from beer to Coke, then from Coke to water. Meat to soup to kittles and bits. Trying to cheer dying spouses and friends, and convince themselves, with words like "better than New York!"

Florida is, after all, the land where people go to die. By the millions, they seem to believe that a few extra degrees of warmth, a palm tree or two, and the occasional glimpse of the ocean will inspire them to live long and prosper. It doesn't work, folks. It just gives the Grim Reaper more to choose from.

But that part of Miami Beach is hidden by the glitz and glamour of the beachfront. On the shore, all is wealth and riches and paparazzi and happiness bought and paid for. With interest. It's a life of doormen and security guards, delivered groceries and glam dinners out, club-hopping and watching the Beautiful People drift in and out. On the shore, life still has hope and a future. The black despair of the past is kept inland a few blocks, in those hot and humid cellblocks of death.

The Hotel Fountainbleu is a frumpy outpost of the old Miami Beach swimming in a neon, Deco sea of modernism. I already dislike New York City and the Fountainbleu is simply a chunk of Manhattanism moved south. It is loud and brassy and brusque and over-expensive. It is guys with lots of gold chains around their necks, white glossy loafers and broads with black bouffant do's, ostentatious dangly bracelets dripping with diamonds, loud voices, and enormous bosoms crammed into hideous bathing attire. There is lots of rude finger-snapping and and competitive oneupsmanship going on at the Fountainbleu. No thanks.

Honie led me through the cacophony of the lobby, through the back doors and out to the huge swimming pool. One side of the pool is a fake-stone grotto, with a swim-up bar inside the cave and a water slide for the kids. Whoopee.

We strolled out to the beach. Honie arranged for a cabana, paying an obscene amount of cash to a handsome hunk, ordered two extra-large pina coladas, stripped down to her bathing suit and lathered up with sunblock. I enjoyed watching. I parked my chair in the shade of the cabana – no sense overdoing the sun—stretched out on the padded chaise and prepared to get acquainted with the inside of my eyelids. The warm morning sun beat down on the beach and a gentle breeze ruffled the flags around us. The warmth, the sun and the sound of the gentle surf, as well as the overdose of Scotch the night before, made me feel deeply lethargic and listless.

"Okay, Hacker," Honie said when she finished laying on the goop and had settled herself in the sun. "Give."

"Eh?" I murmured. I was watching a particularly interesting number in a purple string bikini strolling down the surf line and thinking that even if I wanted to give chase, my body would probably refuse to get up.

"What have you learned about our big happy family?" she asked. "Knowing you, you've probably tripped over some of the skeletons in our closet."

"Is this an official enquiry?" I asked.

"No, you shit." She frowned at me. "It's a question from a friend who wants to compare notes. Remember, I'm in marketing, or will be one day. I want to know if our public imagine matches up with the reality of our product."

"Well," I mused. "I have discovered that Big Wyn has developed some rather interesting management techniques over the years."

"Delicately put," Honie agreed.

"Tell me," I said. "Does she sleep with every golfer on the tour?"

"I can't answer that," Honie said. "My impression is, only with those she wants."

"Like Julie Warren?" I asked.

"Yes, well, Julie is part of Wyn's inner circle," Honie answered. "Some of the girls call them Wyn's Mafia. There are about six of them. Some are appointed to the players' council, some aren't. I don't know if they all take turns in Wyn's bed, and I don't really care. But all of them are pretty loyal to her and will do pretty much anything she asks them to."

"Such as?"

"Oh, mostly stuff like making promotional appearances, taking a sponsor out for a round of golf, doing interviews. Favors, errands, special tasks."

"And how does the beautiful Casey Carlyle fit into this chummy little picture?" I asked.

"Her official title is travel secretary," Honie told me. "Makes all the arrangements to help everyone get to the next stop. She finds rooms and cars and airplane seats for those who need them. Unofficially, she's considered to be Wyn's eyes and ears, and those who aren't part of Wyn's Mafia don't trust her."

"A cold heart in that warm body?" I said. "What a pity."

Honie just shook her head at me,

"I'm not sure the golfing public is aware of the degree of, er, control that Big Wyn exercises over the affairs of the LPGA," I said.

"But it's also true that she has not received the proper credit for all the things she's been able to accomplish," Honie said loyally. "Since she's been president, purses have gone way up, the number of tournaments has increased and we've attracted the best players from all over the world. She has uncanny business instincts and she's been able to pull off some deals no one else – man or woman—has. I've got to give her a lot of credit for that. Benton Bergmeister, in case you haven't noticed, is a zero from the word go. But we need a man, apparently, to schmooze with the inner circle of sponsors and advertisers. That seems to still be a man's world. But Big Wyn …OK, she can be a royal bitch and she's had to step on some toes. But that's what a lot of women in business have to do in order to succeed."

"Oh, c'mon," I protested. "That's bullshit."

We were interrupted by a gaggle of photographers. They were calling out posing directions to a group of LPGA golfers who had suddenly appeared on the scene, posing on the beach with the ocean as backdrop. About half were dressed in golf outfits, the others were in swimwear. Honie and I watched in silence as the publicity juggernaut rolled on.

"Can you imagine a group of PGA Tour players volunteering to spend a few hours posing on the beach to promote their weekend tournament?" Honie asked me.

"Not in a zillion years," I responded, shaking my head in wonder.

"Exactly," she said with some heat. "They throw money at the men, beat down the doors to do things for them. But we have to hustle to sell our product. Now you could say that it's not really fair ... Women professionals play the sport just as well as the men. But that's not the point. Women just have to work harder than men to get up to the same point."

"I don't know—" I started to argue with her some more.

"Oh, c'mon," she said. "It's the same in any business. You hire a man, you automatically assume that he can do the job. All you do is give him an office, a desk and especially a secretary, and you leave him alone to do the work. You hire a woman, on the other hand, and there's always a question about whether she can cut it. There's always that unspoken need for her to prove herself, over and over."

"You're damn right!" agreed a voice behind us. I looked around and saw Mary Beth Burke, dressed in her golf clothes, standing with arms crossed.

"Oh shit," I said. "Outnumbered!"

The photographers, who had now attracted a crowd of onlookers hoping to see some half-naked models or at least a Grade B celebrity, had moved on, back up the beach toward the hotel. Mary Beth pulled off her visor, sank down on the end of my chaise and mopped her brow.

"How'd you manage to escape the sideshow?" I asked.

"Years of practice," she answered with a sigh. She looked over at Honie. "You're the new PR girl, aren't you?" Honie nodded. "Sounds like we finally got one with a head on her shoulders," Burkey said. Honie beamed.

A waitress came up and I ordered a drink for Mary Beth and another round of pina coladas for Honie and me. My first one had mysteriously disappeared in about three gulps.

"We were discussing the various aspects of the weaker sex," I said when the waitress left.

"You mean men," Burkey said slyly, winking at Honie. They laughed together, compatriots.

"Har de har har," I said. "Okay, the theorem on the table is that in today's world, women have to work harder than men to get ahead."

"Agreed," Burkey said,

"But we have not addressed the question as to whether or not women are entirely suited to the fires of competition," I said.

"Oh, my God," Honie groaned. "What year is this? I thought we had worked that all out a few generations ago. C'mon, Hacker, get with the program!"

"No, wait a minute," Mary beth held up a hand. "I want to hear this. Hacker is no pig. At least, I don't think he is. I've always believed he had a brain in there somewhere. Let's hear it, Hacker. But it better be good."

"Okay," I said. "Here goes. We've proved beyond a shadow of a doubt that women are just as smart, just as capable, just as intelligent as men. They can do anything men can do, whether it's brain surgery or playing professional golf. Except, of course, they can't pee standing up."

The two women groaned simultaneously. I laughed and continued.

"But I've got this theory that says being competitive, as women must be in business and on the golf course, cuts across the grain of their womanhood and exacts something of a psychic price. Look, no matter how intelligent and so-phisticated we think we humans are, we're still animals deep down, and our behaviors are still controlled by basic in-stincts—the need for food, shelter and to reproduce the spe-cies. When *Homo* first became *sapiens*, a certain separation of function developed between males and females. Men's bod-ies developed in such a way as to support physical exertion, so they could hunt and gather and provide the food. Women, on the other hand, were assigned the task of birthin' the babies and keeping the home fires burning, literally speak-ing. Men hunted and women nurtured, and their bodies and minds developed for those tasks."

I paused. Honie and Mary Beth were watching me with narrowed eyes, like hungry tigers waiting for their prey to move out of cover so they could pounce. But they still weren't sure in which direction I was going. So they waited. Ready to jump and bring me down to earth.

"So I think that now, even millions of years later, the brain of every woman still contains a tiny little cell or two that keeps emitting this weak signal. Kind of like a satellite way out in space somewhere sending its signal back to earth. And it keeps saying 'nurture…nurture…nurture.'"

"So what you're saying is that we should all be barefoot and pregnant just like God intended?" Honie snapped at me angrily. "You aren't gonna go all religious right on us are ya?"

The waitress came back with her tray of drinks. I passed a frosty glass over to Mary Beth and another to Honie. I restrained myself from challenging them to a chugalug con-test, inasmuch as I was trying to impress them with my eru-dition at the moment.

"No, no," I protested. "What I'm saying is that I guess I agree with what you were saying earlier. Women do have to work harder to succeed. Why? Because they have to overcome not only all the obstacles that society throws in their way, but, more importantly, they have to overcome that little primordial radio signal inside their own heads that's telling them they're not supposed to be out here slaying the saber-tooth tigers. That voice that says 'it's not your job, honey.'"

The two women mulled on that for a while. I did a little work on my drink, fishing around for the maraschino cherry. It went down smooth, out there in the hot sun.

"Burkey," I said, turning to my friend and wiping away my colada-foam mustache. "Generally speaking, what's the weakest part of a professional woman's golf game?"

"The short game," she said quickly. "Chipping and putting."

"Exactly," I said. "And why is that?"

"Because they don't practice that part of the game as much," Honie answered for Mary Beth. "Most women have to work so hard on getting more distance, they just don't have time to practice the short shots."

"Bullshit," I said. "Chipping and putting should be the best part of their games. Look, woods and irons require physical exertion, muscle strength and power. Those are all male attributes, not female. The short game is all about feel and touch and rhythm. Those are 'feminine' words. Putting doesn't require brute strength, it takes touch. So why don't professional women putt better than men?

"Because," I answered my own question, "It's where you close the deal. You know that old cliché…drive for show, putt for dough. The putting green is where one thrusts the spear into your opponent's heart, where you plug him between the eyes, shove him off the cliff or run him over with your tank. Now men have no trouble with that psychic part of the game, because we have our own little radio signals buried deep in our brains. Except ours say 'kill the mother.' Our subconscious is all set up and ready to plunge the dagger in."

I thought a moment, and continued.

"But a woman's little inside voice is saying things like 'Oh, dear. If you sink this puitt than poor Jane will feel badly for having lost. And I'm supposed to make everyone feel good like the nurturing woman I was born to be.' So she yanks the putt left or leaves it short. Which is why women have trouble being competitors."

There was a long moment of silence there on the beach. The young lovely in the purple thong walked by and smiled at me. I smiled back. Not bad, I thought to myself, not bad at all. Hacker's theory of the universal nurturing woman. I liked it.

"That is about the most preposterous amalgamation of bullshit I have ever heard in my entire life," Mary Beth Burke said finally. I smiled at her, too.

"Can't dispute it, though, can you?" I said. "Try this one. Why are lesbians so prevalent in professional atethics? I will assume that neither of you will deny that obvious observation?"

They both nodded, but without any enthusiasm.

"Golf and tennis have always been acceptable sports for women to play," Honie noted.

I nodded. "True," I said. "But when you talk about professional sports, you're not talking about country-club activities. We're talking about sports as vocation. And professional athletics is not something women are traditionally encouraged to do. Girls are supposed to be nice and quiet and attractive. They're not supposed to be able to rifle a two-iron in to a protected pin."

"You may have something there, Hacker,' Mary Beth allowed. "Lord knows I took a ration of shit from my friends and family growing up. My mom gave me dolls and tea sets every birthday, but I just wanted to play with my dad's old set of clubs, or go punt the football or something. Drove her nuts!"

"Okay," I said, "So are lesbians attracted to sports, or do sports attract lesbians? My theory says it's because the successful female athlete has found a way to overcome that little radio signal in her head. She's learned, or maybe doesn't even have, to overcome that natural inclination to be a nurturer, and thus is free to compete without guilt. In effect, she's learned to become a man: competitive, hungry, aggressive, a hunter. For whatever reason, her natural female inclinations disappear."

I was rolling now. Mary Beth and Honie seemed to be engrossed, paying close attention. I took another healthy gulp from my drink and continued.

"So it's only logical to presume that sometimes this unfemaleness will spill over into other areas of her life, such as her sexuality," I said. "She becomes a male aggressor and a sexual aggressor, and seeks a soft, nurturing partner. Hence, she is attracted to women. Simple, really."

I tossed back the last of my drink. The Doctor has spoken. My two women friends said nothing at first. Then they turned to one another.

"I'm not sure, but I think Hacker just called me a bull dyke," Mary Beth said.

"I think I need another drink," Honie said. "Let's go get some lunch."

They didn't say anything to me. I figured I had 'em licked. Blinded by my genius. Honie gathered up her beach things and we walked back toward the hotel. I was a few steps ahead as we passed the huge pool, still feeling proud of my reasoning powers and philosophical understanding of womankind.

Until they each grabbed me by an arm and flung me, decisively, into the pool. Proving yet again that there is nothing so dangerous as a hungry female tiger waiting to pounce on her unsuspecting prey.

TEN

When we got back from the beach there was an envelope stuck under my door. It was from the hotel manager, telling me politely that inasmuch as the Ladies Professional Golf Association had declined to honor the charges for my room, would I be so kind as to contact the front desk and make other arrangements. Screw you, too, I thought, and felt my stomach go sour.

I took a long shower and a longer nap. It was dark when I awoke, First thing I saw was that obsequious letter from the manager, and I decided what I needed more than anything in the world was a drink. I dressed casually – no socks – and went downstairs.

I stopped by the front desk and let them take an imprint of my newspaper's credit card. I could almost feel a collective sigh of relief from the other side of the counter, although all I saw and heard were polite smiles. Loose ends make hoteliers very nervous, and until they have your credit card imprint on file in their hot little hands, you are a loose end.

I headed for my favorite bar off the main lobby. It was getting late and most of the other guests had already headed off to dinner somewhere. I felt like having a liquid meal instead, and ordered up a Scotch on the rocks. I surveyed the room and saw about a half-dozen other customers, talking quietly, heads together. And far off in the corner, all by his lonesome, sat Benton Bergmeister.

He was on a bender. At first glance, you couldn't tell, but I'm an experienced bar watcher and I could see the signs. He was sitting too rigidly straight, for one. People drinking casually are relaxing. They cross their legs, lean on the table or bar, swing their feet. Their bodies are at ease. Benton looked like he was sitting on the end of a long, brass fireplace poker. He was sitting ramrod straight and his forearms formed a perfect ninety-degree angle to his upper arm as they rested symmetrically on the table. His legs were also carefully placed under the table as if he were posing for an artist. Serious, experienced drunks often look like this. They work so hard to present the appearance of sobriety, so no one will notice them, that they begin to look wooden and contrived. It is one of the signs.

Bergmeister also had two glasses in front of him, another giveaway. One was virtually empty, just ice cubes and a lemon peel. The other was untouched and full to the rim. The waitress had probably tried to take away the empty one when she had brought over the new drink, but he had stopped her, saying there was one sip left. People think drunks are messy and sloppy, but the serious ones are as precise as accountants. I knew that Bergmesiter would carefully suck the last vestige of alcohol from the surface of each one of those leftover ice cubes, and then carefully pour the melted water into his new drink. Not a drop to be wasted. Only when the glass was completely empty of any discernable liquid would Benton allow the waitress to carry it away.

This also allowed the drinker to expand the time between drinks so that, again, he could present to the watching world the appearance of pacing his drinking. Only the emotionally distraught drinker will slam down shots one after the other, not caring what people might think. The studious drunk will always take his sweet time making his way into oblivion.

I knew all these secrets after years of experience watching some of Boston's best drunks. I knew, therefore, as I grabbed my drink and headed over to his corner table, that when I sat down he would first be startled, then perplexed as he tried to recognize and place my face. Then he would be overly effusive in greeting me to try and cover up that alcohol-haze-induced lapse.

Right again.

"Hi, Benton," I said affably as I sat down opposite him. "Mind if I join you?"

He jumped. Lurched, really, startled out of whatever private reverie he had been in. He turned his rheumy eyes on me and stared for the long count. *Who the crap is this? Oh, yeah. Hinker. Holder. Hackley. No...that's not right... Oh yeah.*

"Hacker," he said thickly. "So nice to see you again. Have a drink?"

Pretty good. The old coot wasn't totally in the bag...just about halfway there, by my reckoning.

"Got one already," I informed him, holding my glass up for his inspection. He turned his head to look, then turned it back. "So what's new?"

"New?" he repeated dully. "New? Ah, Mr. Hacker, until today there was nothing new in my world. Just the old…as in the same old bullshit. But, I am glad to say, there is about to be a whole vista of new in the world of Benton T. Bergmeister."

Wow. The old guy on the juice was pretty eloquent. Too bad he was totally unintelligible.

"Well, that's great, Benton," I said. "But what exactly are you saying?"

He took a good-sized pull from his glass, the full one, then dumped the remaining contents of his empty one into the full one to replace the booze he had just consumed. I'll bet he was calculating the exact number of milliliters. He glanced around the nearly empty bar and leaned over towards me conspiratorially.

"Can you keep a secret?" he asked in a stage whisper.

I leaned back and gave him my best winning smile. "Secret is my middle name," I told him.

He straightened up and raised his bushy gray eyebrows in surprise.

"Is it now?" he said. "'Secret' Hacker? That's a strange name."

He took another healthy dollop of booze and thought it over. I could imagine his turgid, swollen brain cells trying to process the information, and all his imaginary brainscreen would give him back would be 'syntax error.' I waited while he tried to think. Eventually he gave up and remembered his secret.

"I am resigning as the commissioner of the Ladiesh Perfessional Golfing Ashociation," he announced grandly, putting some drama into his slurred words. He sat back and waited for my stunned and surprised cries to say it wasn't so. I kept silent instead and after an uncomfortable pause, he looked at me with some disappointment. It wasn't the reaction he had hoped for.

"Finally got tired of the bullshit, eh?" I said finally.

It was like I had clicked a switch that released something deep inside the man. Even as heavily boozed up as he was, Bergmeister's tank emptied with a rush, and he spoke to me without any pretense.

"Ain't that the truth?" he gushed. "Ain't that the goddam'dest truth? You will never know the crap I have had to put up with in this job. Incredible."

"How long have you been commissioner?" I asked.

"Seven and a half years, Hacker," he said somewhat sadly. "Seven and one half long and trying years. I still don't know why they hired me. I was with the network in sales, you know, and was looking forward to retiring in another few years. I guess Wynnona figured I could help obtain a better TV deal for the Tour."

"Did you," I asked.

"It's not bad," he said. "Could have been better. But I had very little to do with it. Wynnona Stilwell thought she could do it better. Woman negotiates with the best of them. Brass balls. Brass fuckin' balls, the woman has."

"She must be hell on wheels to work for," I commented.

"I have a bleeding peptic ulcer," Bergmeister told me, looking at me with pitiful eyes. "I'm taking six different kinds of medications. Every drink I take could be the one that kills me. Can I stop? Can I heal? Not so long as that woman continues to rule my life. I am a wreck. Can't sleep. Can't eat. I have had enough."

"Why did you wait so long?" I wondered.

"Hah!" he snorted. "That's what everyone says. 'Why don't you just quit, Benton? Why don't you tell her off? Just leave!' they say. Hah! You just don't understand. You don't just work for that woman. She has to own you, lock, stock and barrel."

"Nobody owns you, Benton," I said. "I think there's a constitutional amendment against it. You either let her push you around like that for all these years, or she's blackmailing you. And that's illegal, too."

His back straightened. "I do not get pushed around," he said gruffly, but with some pain in his voice. He turned his eyes on me and I had to look away. There was pain in those eyes, too, and I couldn't bear to look.

"I can see you don't believe me," he whispered. "No one believes me. The woman is evil."

"Evil?" I echoes. "That's a pretty strong word, Benton."

"Not strong enough," he claimed, shaking his head dolefully. "The woman is a manipulator. It's not enough that she holds all the reins of power. She must control everything, every little detail. No decision, no matter how small, can be made without her approval. Any revenue source must include something for her. She doesn't manage this Tour, she dominates it. It's a need she has…"

His voice tailed off sadly. He stared into his glass, his thoughts far, far away. Finally, he sat up with a jolt and took another sip.

"What did she have on you, Benton?" I asked quietly. If I hadn't heard Mary Beth Burke's story of Big Wyn's vicious episode with young Carol Acorn, I wouldn't have asked the question. But I was beginning to understand something about Big Wyn's management techniques.

"Wh-what do you mean?" he stammered.

His response told me I was on the right track. I zeroed in.

"Benton," I said. "You've been here more than seven years. Nobody with any dignity would take that much crap from somebody like Big Wyn. Like you said, you were ready to retire when you took this job. So I'm guessing you stuck it out only because you had to. She had something on you. What was it?"

He took another long drink before answering. This time, he pretty much drained his cocktail. Instantly, the waitress appeared and Benton nodded affirmatively. She disappeared.

"I'll tell you," he said when she left. He turned toward me with a sigh of what had to be relief. His hands were shaking slightly and color had some up in his face. He seemed anxious to spill something, to someone. And it was more than just the booze talking. Benton Bergmeister had a Lake Meade-sized pool of anguish built up inside, walled in by his own personal Hoover Dam. He had been longing for a way to punch a hole in that dam for a long time and let the truth come gushing out through whatever thick, reinforced walls had been built. He now felt that he could safely do so, and I was the lucky one, or unlucky, to be close at hand when he broke through. And that was now.

"I'll tell you," he cried again. "I've needed to tell someone for a long time."

"Is this off the record?" I interrupted. Normally, if a guy wants to spill his guts, youy let him and figure out later what you can publish and what you can't. But I didn't want to take advantage of Benton's alcoholic state.

He thought for a minute. "Aw, screw it," he said finally. "I don't care what you print about that bitch. She deserves everything she gets."

Benton took one last fortifying swallow of his drink and prepared to let the waters flow.

Suddenly, there was a high-pitched scream from outside the bar, followed by a hysterical cry for help. Bergmeister was frozen to his chair by the effects of his nine or ten drinks, but I leapt to my feet and ran out to the hallway outside the bar, where the door led to the outside patio.

A well-dressed matron in a blue satin dress was standing there, her fist held to her shocked, gaping mouth. She was staring out the double glass doors. A long, red smear of blood on one of the doors led downward to the figure of a slumped heap on the walkway outside. The heap was Honie Carlton.

ELEVEN

I got to Honie first, while behind me I heard someone say "Get an ambulance...fast!"

She lay on her back on the sidewalk, her all-American face gray with shock and creased by rivulets of blood. Kneeling, I felt for a pulse on her neck. When I felt the steady beat, relief washed over me. She was hurt, but not in any immediate danger. The blood was pouring from a couple of nasty gashes on her temple and scalp, and I could see a bluish welling beginning to rise on her left cheekbone. Her eyes were closed and when I gently lifted an eyelid, I could see her eyeballs had rolled backwards into her head. That was not a good sign.

My examination was halted when I was unceremoniously jerked away by two extra-strong hands. They belonged to a heavy-set man dressed inconspicuously in khakis and a

JAMES Y. BARTLETT **103**

white, short-sleeved oxford. The walkie-talkie affixed to his belt told me who he was: hotel security.

He made the same kind of cursory examination of Honie's vital signs that I had, pulled his handset from its leather clip and spoke a few soft words into it. Almost simultaneously, I heard the soft bleating of a siren in the distant night air. The security guy look around at the small crowd of aghast guests that had gathered.

"It's okay folks," he said calmly, holding Honie's head off the ground. "Help's on the way. Go on, now. Give us some room here. Thanks."

Some other hotel personnel ran up and helped push the crowd back inside the glass doors. Standing in the doorway, peering out with her hand to her mouth in a pose fo shock, was Casey Carlyle. I watched as she turned and sped down the hallway towards the lobby.

The security guy turned to look at me when I didn't move away with the rest. "Husband?" he asked.

"Friend," I said. "She's with the LPGA. Name's Honie Carlton."

"She staying here?" the guy asked. I nodded. He pulled his walkie talkie out again and passed on the news. I could imagine the fast telephone call that would be made to the general manager. Hotel guest assaulted outside main building. Possible liability suit. Get down here fast and begin damage control.

"Get lots of muggings around here?" I asked.

The security guy cocked an eye at me, but after a moment's pause, shook his head. "Very unusual," he said. "Neighborhood around here's not too good, but we hardly ever get bad guys in here. We have cameras and sensors all over the place. We'll close the place down tight and do a perimeter search. If there's a perp hiding out there –" he motioned out at the golf courses, "—we'll find him." All the time he was talking, I noticed that he was carefully attending to Honie. He made sure her airways were unclogged and that she could breath. He held her head just above the hard concrete of the sidewalk and had pulled out a handkerchief to try and wipe some of the blood from her face.

The siren got louder as it whooped up to the hotel and within minutes, two paramedics burst through the glass doors. They took over from the security guy, made yet another quick examination and radioed in Honie's vital statistics to a hospital emergency room. They moved with efficiency and skill, and the security guy and I backed off and watched.

"Don Collier," the security guy said, holding out his hand. "I'm with the hotel."

I told him my name and we shook hands. "I'm going with her," I told him. "She's an old friend. I'm also staying here at the hotel." I told him my room number.

Two more paramedics arrived with a stretcher, and accompanied by three management-types from the hotel. Collier pulled them off into a corner and briefed them. He spoke a few more times into his walkie-talkie.

As they lifted her onto the stretcher, Honie groaned once, softly. I grabbed her hand and squeezed. I followed the crew back through the lobby and out to the entrance. It took a bit of arguing, but eventually they let me ride in the ambulance to the hospital. I think they saw the look in my eyes.

On the ride in, one of the medics riding in back with me telephoned in to the hospital.

"Mobile Three," he said. "We've picked up the Doral call. White female, approximately 25 years old. Contusions and apparent concussion. Loss of blood minimal. Possible fractures to ribs, collarbone, upper arms. Blood pressure steady. Breathing normal. Over." He looked up at me.

"They'll have a neurologist standing by and get the orthopedist on call to come check her out for broken bones. I don't think anything major is busted, but her breathing is a little wheezy, which could mean a broken rib or two. She'll be okay."

He looked down at her as the ambulance weaved through traffic.

"World's going to hell when they start attacking guests at the Doral," he said. "Druggies know where the money's at, though. All those rich tourists are like sitting ducks for them. And the druggies don't give a damn how it looks for the Chamber of Commerce."

He bent down over Honie and listened again to her breathing through a stethoscope. Her eyelids flickered open briefly and another soft moan escaped from her lips. I reached across the cramped aisle of the ambulance and grabbed her hand. It felt cold and limp and lifeless.

"Hey, kid," I said softly. "It's Hacker. You're gonna be okay. We're on the way to get you an aspirin or something, so just hold on."

Her eyes flicked open and she turned her head to look at me as through a thick and enveloping fog.

"Murr," she said thickly, trying to sit up. The paramedic and I gently pushed her back down. "*Murr,*" she said again, insistently. "*Wampy…hernninon…bulldosh.. farrinch.*" Her eyes closed again and she was silent for the rest of the ride.

"They sometimes are like that after a concussion," the medic said. "It's normal. She'll be okay."

At the hospital, I was politely but firmly held back while they wheeled Honie out of sight into the bowels of the emergency room. The paramedic who'd been driving took me to an orderly who took me to a nurse who took me to a small office where I was forced to spend half an hour answering questions posed by a bored clerk in front of a computer screen. I knew the answers only to about half the questions, and when I began to wonder in a loud voice if they were withholding medical services for lack of answers to a bunch of stupid questions, and whether they were prepared for some major-league malpractice suits, they finally led me back to her curtained-off room.

There, a slightly harried doctor of Asian descent assured me that Honie was stable, breathing well and would be held overnight for observation. Nothing broken, nothing damaged, pretty good concussion resulting from a beating. All precautionary tests had been ordered, results would be studied later that night and again in the morning. Patient had been medicated for pain and would sleep comfortably and deeply through the night. Come back in the morning, Mr. Hacker, sir, and she should be able to hold a conversation with you. But not now.

So I taxied back to the Doral and went searching for Don Collier. The security office was housed in a mobile trailer, a boxy, prefab structure well hidden behind the main hotel structure. Wooden stairs led up to the trailer's door and a latticelike molding had been nailed into place around the base to disguise the concrete blocks upon which the building rested. Going up the three stairs, I could feel the whole building shake.

Inside, Collier was alone, sitting at a cheap metal desk, talking on his telephone. The air inside was hot and stale and smelled of burnt coffee. Behind the door, I notioced a blackened glass globe coffee pot, with a half-inch of acidic brew curdling inside.

Collier's desk was military neat and mostly empty. The desk took up most of the width of the trailer. Behind it were a couple of beat-up file cabinets and a row of TV monitors, each showing a different view of some public area of the hotel. Red lights winked off and on below the monitors, on which the pictures changed periodically. Most of the cameras were showing doorways.

Collier hung up the phone and looked up at me.

"Nice digs," I said.

He looked around and shrugged. "Not much sense making like Donald Trump," he said. "No one much comes in here except me and my men. All we do is try and keep it clean. How's the girl?"

"She's sleeping it off," I told him. "Nothing broken except her head. Any news on this end?"

He shook his head. "Negative," he said. "No witnesses as far as I can find, no sign of any nonlocals. We swept the golf courses and only found one couple engaged in nonauthorized activity on thirteen green of the Gold course."

"Nonauthorized activity?" I asked.

"Screwing like bunnies," Collier grinned at me. "Let's just say we scared the pants back on 'em." He laughed. "These conventioneers can come up with the strangest places to make whoopee. Never figured out why they want to roll around in pesticides and get their privates attacked by bugs when we have some of the most comfortable beds in the world. But hey—" he shrugged, "The customer is always right."

His phone rang and I watched the changing views of doors and entrances while he spoke briefly.

"I personally checked around that courtyard where Miss Carlton was assaulted," he said after he hung up. "Nothing there I could see, but I'll take another look after sunrise. I did find Miss Carlton's things, however."

He turned to a little cabinet behind his desk and pulled a notebook binder and Honie's pocketbook out of the top drawer. The binder was one of those bulky, daily calendar efficiency things, with colored tabs and preprinted sheets designed to help workaday types organize and plan every last facet of their lives. I have a deep and long-standing aversion to the damn things. I don't like to look at a blank page and worry about thinking up enough things to do to fill up an entire day. I don't like to preplan my life down to the quarter hour. I prefer to let life happen. I like to do what I feel like doing. I don't like being made to feel guilty if all I can think of to do is two things in a day, leaving all those extra lines blank. I don't like seeing all those empty lines as representative of my pathetic attempt at a life. Besides, I've never seen one of those damn things that had a space on it labeled "Break to take a leak." Guess that's not an efficient way to spend one's time.

"Mind if I take a look?" I asked Collier. He nodded his assent, so I picked up the notebook and began to leaf through it. I found the section for today's activities. Honie was apparently one of those hyperorganized persons, but I decided not to hold that against her. Looking back through the last few days of her calendar, I saw her scribbled notations, phone numbers and messages, and appointments listed in her neat handwriting. Some of her entries were in some kind of personal shorthand code, and others had been crossed out, apparently when the task had been accomplished.

"Hacker A. 4:30 p.m. Flt. #478."

"Cocktails, 7:30. Wyn's suite. Send dress out for cleaning."

I remembered when Honie had been dismissed from the gathering that first night and my heart went out to her. I flipped over to today's activities. Once back from the beach, her afternoon had been a busy one. She had apparently met with several of the local TV news crews and sports writers doing interviews, distributed a handful of publicity photos of some of the players, checked on supplies for the press room and called ahead to the next tournament stop, in Sarasota, for some advance work. There was also a penciled notation at the bottom of the page that caught my eye.

"Julie W. 5:30. Bring pub.cal."

"Did you see this?" I asked Collier, showing him the notation. "It looks like it was added after the rest of the day's tasks. Everything else on this page is written in ink."

Collier nodded. "Already checked it out," he said. "Julie W. is Julie Warren, one of the players. She's also on the player's committee and she told me that she had asked Miss Carlton to discuss some future publicity plans for the next few tournaments. 'Pub.cal' stands for 'publicity calendar.' She said they met for about forty-five minutes in the Players' Lounge, then went their separate ways. Miss Carlton was assaulted an hour later. Miss Warren says she went back to her room after the meeting and took a shower."

I shrugged and went back to Honie's daily calendar. But I couldn't find anything else that might indicate who or why. Still, I recalled uneasily, Honie's description of Big Wyn's Mafia included Julie Warren. Had Big Wyn sent Julie to beat Honie up? Even with what I knew about Big Wyn's style, I doubted that.

"Let me know if anything turns up," I told Collier. "Somebody whacked the hell out of that girl and I'd like to find out who."

"You and me both, pal," he said.

Walking back through the lobby on my way to my room, I was intercepted by Casey Carlyle. She was wearing conservative slacks and a cashmere sweater.

"Oh, Hacker, there you are," she said, gushing a bit as she grabbed my arm. "I understand you went to the hospital with Honie. Is she OK? Is she badly hurt? Did she say who did this terrible thing?"

I look for a moment into her cool blue eyes. Her words indicated a normal concern for a fellow employee, but her eyes were dead and flat, as they had been the night of Wyn's cocktail party. I got the sense I was being pumped for information. But I smiled at her and patted her shoulder reassuringly.

"Oh, she's been hurt pretty bad," I said, "But the doctor says she'll be fine. Nobody knows what happened yet. They'll try and talk to her in the morning."

"Oh, thank goodness," Casey exhaled. "I'll go and tell Wynnona."

She turned and took her beautiful self away in gliding, graceful steps, her long blond hair streaming behind her. Call me a cynic, but as she went I wondered to myself if she was going to tell Bug Wyn that Honie wasn't badly injured, or that Honie hadn't yet identified her assailant.

TWELVE

I woke up early the next morning, troubled and restless. I had been having a dream, one of those not-quite-night mares, but strange and disturbing nonetheless. I had been in a conference room heavily appointed in mahogany paneling and brass fixtures, with gilded portraits on the walls. Sitting around the long, walnut table with me had been Wynnona Stilwell, Mary Beth Burke, Benton Bergmeister, Carl the resplendently pith-helmeted doorman, Julie Warren, Carol Acorn, Casey the Delicious Dyke dressed in an off-the-shoulder shimmering black dress, and I think Ronald Reagan, who was catnapping at the far end of the conference table.

We had been sitting around debating the real meaning of the words "murr, wampy, herrninon, bulldosh and farrinch," which was what Honie had said to me in the ambulance the night before. The discussion, I recalled, had been quite heated at times. Reagan woke up at one point and tried to get a word in, but no one would let him speak.

Suddenly, the heavy double doors had swung wide open and Honie Carlton had walked in, wrapped head to tie in as much gauze as an Egyptian mummy. Though muffled by the bandages, her voice had sounded amused. "You are all being quite silly," she had said. "I said the damn words. The meaning is perfectly clear."

She was about to translate for us when I woke up. I got out of bed and stood for a while at the window in my room, curtains pulled back so I could stare out at the soft, early-morning light that was just beginning to give some definition to the trunks of the trees and shapes of the oleander shrubs. With the first hints of light came life, with the first songs of the birds and the buzzing of insects as they began their daily struggle for survival.

The early morning is always melancholy for me. Some feel the same way about midnight or the wee small hours. But for me, it's the dawn. I could almost feel a cold, damp fog licking around my feet, working inexorably upward toward my heart and soul.

I don't know why. Daybreak is supposed to represent yet another victory over darkness and death. But it always seems to me to be a reminder that the darkness is still there, lurking, waiting to return. We all spend so mich time trying to keep that darkness away. But it's all just whistling past the boneyard. Because soon or later, the scary and lurid places that dwell within take over. It's like those contrary ying-and-yang symbols, the happy face and the death-mask grimace. We spend our days imagining our lives are a romantic comedy with Rock Hudson and Doris Day when they're really the bleak and desolate landscape of King Lear, Act III.

I shook myself, dropped the curtains and told myself to snap out of it. Laid the melancholia to the events of the last few days .. the conflict with Big Wyn...the squalid story of Carol Acorn's descent into hell...the brutal attack on my friend Honie.

Action. I dug out a worn and comfortable T-shirt, an old pair of shorts and my beat-up sneakers. I am not a health freak, not do I aspire to ever become one. But sometimes, I run. Jog, really, with lots of breaks for wind-gasping walking. I run not to boast to my friends how many miles a week I can do, nor to try to qualify for someone's memorial 5-K race, nor to get myself into some kind of mythical fighting trim. No, I only run when the spirit moves me, and that comes infrequently. Sometimes I get moved when I look into the mirror and notice the old belly is beginning to sag. Or when I have been a bad boy at the bar and need to sweat the devil alcohol from my system. When I am bored. Or when I need to banish melancholy with physical action. If this kind of exercise happens to provide some other, beneficial, side effects to my overall well being, fine. I could care less. In fact, every time I decide to run, I remember that guy who wrote all those running-is-healthy books who keeled over dead while on a jog one day. I try not to do that. Keel over dead, that is.

Golf courses, not coincidentally, are ideal places to jog, especially early in the morning before anyone else is awake. As I started off down the cart path on one of the fairways, the air was fresh and cool in the soft pink light of dawn. Dew hung heavily on the carpets of green, broken only by the tiny-footed tracks of some nocturnal animals who had scurried across the fairways even earlier than me. I ran down two holes, keeping to the asphalt paths and, after working through the painful bits, settled into a second-wind, steady pace. To get there, I run in cadence with my breathing: two steps per inhale, two steps per exhale. Once you hit that point, your mind is freed from the constant signals to cut this crap out and stop!

I held that pace, admiring the world around me which was beginning to awaken to the new day. Fat mullet flopped out of the ponds I passed, making loud splashes as they fell back into the dark water. Long-legged egrets stood regally in the shallows, waiting patiently for a bold minnow to swim too close and become breakfast. The sun suddenly exploded over the line of windbreak pines to the east in a blazing ball of orange and I felt a warm sweat break out on my arms and shoulders.

Ten minutes later I was way out on the fringe of the Doral property. I had lost track of which hole or even what color course I was on. I spied the figure of a man fishing in one of the retention lakes and jogged over in his direction. As I drew near, I made out the stocky figure of Harold Stilwell, dressed in denim overalls and a fisherman's vest, dotted with all manner of lures and flies. His tackle box was propped open at the base of a nearby tree and Stillwell was casting a plug out into the lagoon with practice flips of his thick, beefy wrists.

"Morning," I called out in a wheezy gasp. "Catching anything?"

He grunted at me, staring at the water as he reeling in his line in short, furious bursts, pausing between each burst to twitch the line with his fingers. I watched. Finally, he sighed and reeled his line up and out of the water.

"They're dickin' with me," he said, turning to me. "There's a big ole bass out here that I caught last year. I sent him back to grow. I know it's the same one, 'cause last year it was the same deal. He spent three days in a row nibblin' at it, spittin' it out n' dickin' with me. Fourth day, finally, the sucker hit it and I got 'im. I laughed in his fool face and sent him back to grow some."

He ran the hook end of his lure through one of the metal eyelets in his rod and reeled the line tight. He bent over and closed the lid of his tackle box, then stood up and looked at me.

"You're that Hacker feller, right?" he asked, looking at me straight in the eye. I nodded. He looked thoughtful. "Gave Wynnona a big-time hissy fit," he said. "Had coffee yet?" I shook my head. He gave me a "follow me" wave and turned.

I followed him around the lake and into a thicket of pines on the other side, In a shady clearning stood a huge motor home, sleek and powerful-looking. VISTACRUISER 98 it said on the outside. The machine was in full camping mode: foldaway steps leading to the side entrance door, canvas awning over the door, aluminum table and folding chairs set up outside. I caught the scent of fresh-brewed coffee drifting in the air.

I laughed out loud. "Wynnona Stilwell lives here?" I asked, unbelieving. "Camping out? Don't the chiggers mess up her swing?"

Stilwell grunted. "Hell, no, you damn fool. She's got that fancy-ass hotel suite she stays in. Me? I can't sleep in those places. Hate air conditioning and I don't like a place where you can't open the goldurn windows. Naw, Wynnona stays up there. Closer to the golf course and all that other stuff she has to do. Me…I like it better out here. More peace and quiet."

"Do you do this at every tournament?" I wondered.

"Well, Wynnona makes sure they find me a good place," he said. "Some places are better'n others. Sometimes I just get a place in the parking lot next to Wyn's hotel, but then I start to feel like a freak at the circus, everyone starin' at me. I like it better out in the open, where I can kick off my shoes. How do you take your coffee?"

I told him black and he disappeared inside the camper, returning shortly carrying two steaming mugs of joe. The orange ball of sun had begun its work of the day, raising the heat and humidity to uncomfortable levels. But here in Stilwell's glen, the shade of the trees retained a bit of the morning's cool comfort.

"Does Wyn ride with you in this thing between tournaments?" was my next question. I was having trouble picturing Big Wyn as the RV sort.

"When she can, when she can," Harold said, settling down into his lounge chair. "There are times when she just needs to get away from it all, so we crank this baby up and head for the nearest nowhere we can find. Do some fishing, listen to the crickets, admire the view…that kinda stuff. Helps get her head back on straight, I think," he said.

"How long have you two been married?"

"Oh, hell, more years than I care to remember," Harold said, laughing a bit. "I owned this little garage outside of Evanston, Indiana, and one fine summer's day here she comes, a smokin' and a coughin'. Like most women, she never bothered much with checkin' on a car's oil. Just kept pumping gas into her until she finally seized up.

"She was heading for a tournament, but in the time it took me to fix up her car, we got to talking.'" Stilwell paused and sipped some coffee, then stared down pensively into the blackness of his cup, as if he could see the events of that long-ago day, the bright cornflower blue of an Indiana summer sky appearing in its inky depths.

"She come back after her tournament, which she won, by the way," he grinned over at me, a lopsided, old man's grin. "One thing led to another, and here we are."

"Sounds like a whirlwind romance," I said. "And it sounds like you give her something she needs."

He nodded at me. "That's what marriage is all about," he said. "I'm her backstopper. She's always been a house afire. Never sits still, always something else to do. But from time to time she needs someone to listen to her bitchin' and moanin' or to have someone she can just kick around and know it don't mean nuthin', or just someone who tells her it's all OK. That's my job."

He said this with just a hint of something deeper behind it. Pain? Anger? Heavy heartedness? I almost held my tongue, but didn't.

"Do you like that job?" I asked.

He harrumphed, and waved my question away as through it were a bothersome mosquito.

"She's a wonderful woman, deep down," he said. "And it's been a wonderful life. Sure as hell better'n spending forty years cleanin' the chich bugs off the Widow Feeney's Chevy."

I sipped my coffee. The insects in the glade began a buzzing sound that ebbed and flowed in atonal harmony.

"How much do you get involved in her LPGA stuff?" I asked.

"Not a whit and thanks to the Good Lord," Harold said vehemently. "All that jawin' and talkin' and meetings and such is all her doin' and she's welcome to it all. I'm a simple man, Hacker, and I'm getting to be an old man and I like my peace and quiet."

"Somehow, I can't quite see being married to Big Wyn Stilwell and being able to find any peace and quiet," I laughed.

"Meanin' what, pard?" he asked, and I noted the undercurrent of malice in his tone. I held my hand in peace.

"Nothing, Harold," I said. "Just that what I see of Big Wyn is a woman in constant motion, juggling seven things at once and always surrounded by a gaggle of people who want something from her. You know...Casey and Julie and Bergmeister."

"Ass-kissers, every one," he snorted derisively. "Bunch a damn ass-kissing parasites, you ask me. That Benton fella's pretty nice, though he drinks too much. He also takes more shit than a country outhouse." He stirred in his chair and drained the last of his coffee.

"But I'll tell ya something, Hacker," he said, shaking a finger at me wisely. "I been out here with Wynnona for nearly twenty years now, and I seen 'em come and seen 'em go. And they all go, sooner or later. Whenever they start lording their fancy asses over this lil ole country boy, I think about that. They might believe they are the cock of the walk, but I know better. Sooner or later, they're history."

He was getting pretty wound up, and I was planning on waiting for more. But just then, a dark green pickup trucked pulled into the glade. The driver blew his horn in greeting and jumped out. Painted on the side of the truck were the words DORAL HOTEL AND CC MAINTENANCE. The driver wore neat green overalls and a broad-billed baseball cap.

"Howdy, Hal!" he hollered. "Ready to tackle that mower engine?"

"Soon enough, soon enough," Stilwell muttered and disappeared inside his camper again. He brought out another mug of coffee and introduced me to Charley Dillon.

"Charley's probably the best mechanic in South Florida," Stilwell told me.

"But I don't know half of what you've already forgot about engines, Hal," Charley said, gulping down his coffee. He looked at me. "Man is a goddam mechanical wizard."

"Ah," I said, "So you still hang around the maintenance shed, eh? Old mechanics never die, right?"

"Hellfire, man," Dillon piped up. "I save up the tough stuff for when I know Hal's gonna be in town. He can get anything motorized humming in nothing flat!"

I laughed and finished my coffee. Stilwell took our cups inside, then locked up the camper and climbed into the pickup with Charley. I waved as they drove away and headed back for the hotel, this time at the slowest pace possible.

Big Wyn and the Backstop. It sounded like the name of a rock group. Relationships come in many varied shapes and colors, I knew, but this one was very strange. Harold was married to Big Wyn, and Big Wyn was married to her job. I couldn't help hearing something of a discordant note when he had talked about his marital "job." I wondered what Harold Stilwell got in return. I wondered if he ever wondered. Wynnona got the freedom to pursue her career and the comfort of having someone to backstop her when times were tough. But who would backstop Harold? How much backstopped was required for a woman as manipulative as Wynnona Stilwell? Did Harold even know about that part of Wyn's life, or was he happily in the dark, out fishing in his lakes and camping under the stars? Did he put his thick, beefy arms around her and say "There, there Wyn, it's OK to step on people's toes and ruin their lives."?

And what about Big Wyn's adventurous sex life? How did Harold Stilwell relate to that? Did he know about it? Did he push it aside because, as he said, he knew that one day they would be history and he'd still be there, by Wyn's side? Or did he just stay in his homey little camper and keep his eyes shut?

It seemed to me that the Wynnona-Harold marriage was one heavily tilted to her side. No surprise there. I began to understand why Harold Stilwell enjoyed camping out, far away from the sound and fury that must be part of a life with Big Wyn. He got his peace and quiet, along with a ration of loneliness, in return for escaping from the rest of the harsh realities of life with Wynnona. I felt sorry for and admired Stilwell at the same time. Not too many of us would have the bullshit quotient he did. If he could deal with the weight of the circumstances of his peculiar life with Big Wyn and still find some measure of happiness, that was admirable. I couldn't do it, and I don't know too many who could.

Well, I thought as I came into view of the hotel, different strokes for different folks. I laughed at my own pun, taken sexually. Then I began to think of Big Wyn in a sexual situation. That's when I realized I was probably suffering from severe oxygen deprivation, or something even more serious, and decided exercise time was over, and breakfast time was nigh.

THIRTEEN

After breakfast I cabbed back over to the hospital. Honie was sitting up in bed, holding an ice pack to her temple. Her eyes were darkly shadowed and she didn't look like she was having a great time.

"Hi gorgeous," I said cheerfully. "Wanna dance?"

She looked at me with eyes of the damned. "Fuck. Off," she enunciated each word clearly. "I want to die."

"Not feeling so hot, huh?"

"Everything I own hurts, plus a few spare parts I didn't even know I had," she said mournfully, and shifted her ice pack to her other temple. A nurse came in, checked her chart, hovered briefly over her bed and then disappeared.

"Christ," Honie said. "There's the pro-am today and I had about seven zillion things to do. And I was supposed to set up some interviews for next week in Sarasota and ..."

"Whoa, girlfirned," I soothed. "Relax, sit back...You aren't going anywhere. You almost got yourself killed last night, so don't worry about bravely carrying on. Isn't there someone else who can do all that stuff?"

"Yeah," Honie admitted, trying to find a comfortable position in bed. "My boss Karla is flying in from Houston this morning. I guess she can handle any emergencies."

"There," I said. "You see? Now tell me about last night. Do you remember anything? Like who it was that beat the tar out of you?"

She groaned. "Not you, too," she moaned. "That hotel guy and the police were in her at the crack of dawn asking me all kinds of questions six different ways."

"And ...?"

"I don't remember a thing," she said sadly. "I remember walking back toward the hotel and thinking how pretty that fountain looked in the pink twilight. Next thing I know, I wake up here with my head about to burst. Oww."

She had shifted position again, and it made her wince. I reached over and squeezed her hand.

"What were you doing before it happened?" I asked.

She lay back and closed her eyes. "I had been meeting with Julie Warren in the players' lounge," she said, her voice tired. "She was giving me a hard time, so I was glad to finally get out of there."

"Hard time about what? You don't work for her, do you?"

She cracked one eye open and looked at me.

"Like I told you, she's on the players' council and is one of Wyn's 'mafia,'" she said. "So that means I do report to her, in a roundabout way. I mean, I'm supposed to report to

Karla, who reports to Benton who reports to Big Wyn and the Players' Council. But it's more like having the board of directors around all the time. All the players are supposedly equal, but some are more equal than others. So I have to suck up to them all."

"So what was last night's third degree about?" I pressed.

"You," Honie sighed.

"Me?"

"Yeah. You know, how could I invite such an asshole like you to come down? What did I think I was doing? Didn't I know anything about you? Didn't I think to have someone approve the plan before I did it? What were my plans to get rid of you? Stuff like that. What a bitch."

"What did you say?"

"I finally told her that my job was to get press coverage for the tour and what the press chose to write about was basically out of my control. And I told her that I'd known you for years and that you were basically OK in my book. Then I packed up my stuff and left."

"So when you left, she was basically pissed?" I pressed.

Honie opened both eyes and looked at me, blinking once. "Well, yeah, I guess so," she said. "But then, Julie's always pissy. After a while, you just ignore it. I was tired of listening to her ranting after half an hour, so I just tuned her out, basically. I had other things more important to do, so I said what I said and left."

She thought for a minute. "But you aren't thinking that maybe Julie was the one who ...?"

Her thought was cut off by the arrival of the doctor, who greeting Honie cheerfully, as doctors are wont to do, then turned and asked me to leave the room. I went out and stood in the hallway, thinking. I remembered the sight of Julie Warren's red and angry face when she had threatened me in the lunch room a few days ago. Julie certainly looked big and strong, but could she have inflicted the damage on Honie? More important, would she? What possible advantage could there be for Big Wyn that would cause her to order one of her own employees beaten up? It didn't add up.

The doctor came out into the hall. "I've ordered another shot of Demerol," he said. "She's still in a lot of pain, so I think we'll keep her here one more day. She's young and healthy, so we should be able to get her out of here by tomorrow."

"Let me ask you something," I said.

"Shoot."

"Do you think she could have been beaten up by another woman?"

"Only a very big or very angry one," he said. "Funny you should ask, though."

"Why?"

"The police asked me that same question two hours ago."

When I got back to the Doral, I went over to the pressroom and found that Julie Warren's pro-am tee time was in about an hour. She was probably over at the practice range warming up, I was told. To get to the range, I had to walk around the back of the hotel, past that fountain that Honie had thought so pretty in the pink twilight before someone concussed her nearly to death. There was no sign of violence today, just neat rows of yellow mums and red coleus, some trimmed box holly and a palm or two for tropical effect.

The practice tee was busy. The women professionals were warming up side-by-side with their amateur partners for the day, who in turn were busy trying to figure out how not to be embarrassed on the golf course today. There was a great deal of camaraderie going on, as the woman pros tried to help their partners find a semblance of a swing.

Most of the amateurs playing in the pro-am were male, as usual, drawn from the ranks of the tournament's sponsors, program advertisers and others connected with the resort. Watching them flail away on the range, I could tell that most of them were twice-a-month golfers. They all seemed to have herky swings that resulted in a lot of topped shots and violent slices. Still, the women pros were trying to help, providing hints and words of encouragement, It was something you don't usually see on the PGA Tour, were the pros pretty much show up because they have to. While some do take the time to be nice, many can't abide pro-ams, and their attitudes show it.

Which reminded me of my favorite pro-am story, featuring a gruff old pro from the Virginia mountains. As was his usual practice, this pro had, after the initial introductions, said nary a word to his playing partners throughout the rest of the round. No stories, no jokes, no "nice shots," or "that's too bad." He was so intimidating, in fact, that the rest of the group just tried to keep out of his way, putting out quickly and moving on to the next tee. It was a miserable day for all of them.

Until the last hole, Walking up to the green, the pro glanced at the scoreboard and noticed that his team was in position to win the event. One of the amateurs had reached the green in regulation and within birdie range, but, following the procedure of the rest of the round, was about to just pick it up in order not to delay the pro's day any further.

"Hold on, son," the pro finally spoke. "If you make that putt, it'll be a net eagle and we can win this thing."

The amateur stopped and looked at the pro, amazed that he had actually spoken.

"What do you mean?" the guy asked.

"You get a stroke here," the pro explained. "Knock that baby in and we'll win."

"What do we win?" the amateur asked next.

"Well, y'all will get some nice prizes and I'll get about a thousand bucks," the pro said.

The amateur nodded. He marked and cleaned his ball. Studied the putt carefully. Took his time. Finally, he was ready. He walked up to the ball, took a couple of careful practice swings. Settled in over the ball. Everyone else fell quiet.

Then he looked up at the pro, standing by the side of the green, gave him an evil smile, and whacked the ball clear off the green and into the nearby lake. "Up yours," he said and walked away.

The stocky figure of Julie Warren was laboring in the next-to-last practice area on the long, wide tee. Dark patches of sweat colored her light-blue shirt and her white visor held back her mass of sweaty black hair. I noticed right away that she was wearing a golf glove on both hands. Unusual. Interesting.

I went and stood directly behind her, standing behind a yellow rope strung some five yards behind her. She was punching low, hooking seven-irons at a flagstick in the distance. She didn't pay any attention to anyone else, so I ducked under the rope and walked closer. Nobody noticed.

"Where'd you learn your boxing skills?" I finally asked out loud.

She jumped a little, turning to see me standing right behind her. Recognizing me, she puffed out a sharp burst of air, then turned back to her practice.

"I figure you must have lots of brothers, you're probably the youngest, so you grew up learning how to defend yourself," I said. I might as well have been speaking to a tree. Julie Warren went back to hitting balls, ignoring me. "They probably taught you the basics and I'll bet you became the playground bully with lots of opportunities to practice. What I want to know is, do you like the feeling of punching someone's face in? The sound of it? The sight of the blood? Which part is it that turns you on?"

She turned to look at me again, her face red and flushed. "What the hell are you talking about, Hacker?" she cried. "Leave me alone."

"When you beat the shit out of Honie, did it give you a sexual thrill?" I continued. "You like beating people? " I was starting to get loud, ignoring the dangerous buzzing sound in my head. I knew I was beginning to lose it, and I sensed some of the other golfers around us had stopped their practice to look our way.

"You're crazy, man," she said, although I saw her cast her eyes nervously down the range. "I had nothing to do with that, and you can't prove I did."

"No," I said, "I don't suppose I can. But I'll bet that if you take off those gloves, we could all see some bruised knuckles. Must be hell on the old grip the next day after you pound someone's face in. How do you hold onto the club?"

I took a half-step towards her. My eyes had narrowed and the sky turned another shade red and ugly. She raised her golf club menancingly above her head.

"You take one more step, shithead, and it'll be the last one," she growled.

We glared at each other. Why is it not nice to hit a woman? They can be as hateful and ugly as men, sometimes worse. And this one, with her stocky shoulders, muscular arms, thick, strong legs ... she was no delicate flower of womanhood. Even if I could get the seven-iron out of her hands before she planted it in my cranium, she would be tough to take. Especially if she did have some boxing or fighting skills, as I suspected. But still I hesitated, for no other reason than the stricture long drilled in, that boys don't hit girls. I think she knew that, because she began to grin at me, an evil, you-can't-touch-me kind of grin. It almost tripped me over the side, again.

"Here, here," said a clipped, British-accented voice behind us. I didn't take my eyes off Julie and her raised weapon. It would have been just her style to clock me one when I wasn't looking. Women can be dirty fighters in a clinch. The voice came into view, and a woman stepped between us. "If you feel you must grapple, I will thank you to do it elsewhere," she said, taking command. "We are trying to practice golf here."

She was a tall woman, dressed in a stylish navy golf skirt and a red-and-white striped polo shirt. Her reddish blond hair was pulled back in a ponytail, revealing a face that, while not pretty in the classic sense, was strong and well defined. She had wide shoulders and a trim, athletic build.

"Julie, please put down that club and stop this nonsense at once," she snapped sternly at my opponent.

Julie obeyed. The woman then turned to me, her eyes flashing with anger. "And you, sir," she said coldly. "This area is reserved for players only. Spectators are limited to areas behind the yellow ropes. Kindly take yourself there. At once!"

Now that Julie had lowered her murder weapon, I could afford to take my eyes off her and take the time to study our mediator in more detail. I decided she was pretty, especially those flashing blue eyes. Even if they were flashing at me.

"Hacker, Boston *Journal*," I said to her. Miss Warren and I were just discussing some alternative uses of a golf club. I believe Miss Warren intends to become an ecological big-game hunter when her days on the Tour are over. Her ideas about clubbing the game into submission are much more sporting than firearms, don't you agree?"

The eyes stopped flashing in anger and began to glitter, and her face broke out in a toothy grin. She opened her mouth and brayed a hearty laugh.

"Ha ha!" she bellowed, "Jolly good! That's the spirit, eh, Julie?"

Julie Warren apparently didn't agree. She turned on her heel, grabbed her other clubs and stalked off, throwing a last evil, hateful glance my way. The laughter of my new friend followed her down the long green range.

"Jolly good line, Hacker," she gasped. "I say, I fear we'll both be in for it now." She stuck out a hand. "Sybil," she introduced herself. "Sybil Montgomery."

I knew the name. She was one of Britain's better woman players and one of a growing contingent of foreign-born players now competing on the U.S. Tour. Unlike the men, who had a successful, big-money tour to play in Europe, women's golf was lagging overseas, so the best players migrated to the U.S. There was the cadre of Swedish stars, trained from youth to compete in athletics; a few French and Italian girls, several Irish, English and Scottish women, and a ton of new arrivals from Japan and Korea.

"C'mon then." Sybil said, grabbing my arm and pulling me away from the practice range, where golf activity had resumed after our brief interruption. "It's lunchtime and I'm famished. Thank God I don't have to play in the pro-am today. You buy lunch."

What else could I do? "Right-o, then," I said. "Off we go!"

She laughed again. It was a sound I was beginning to like.

FOURTEEN

S o," I said when we had filed through the buffet line, loading up with chicken salad, a cold pasta and sliced tomatoes with basil and mozzarella and ensconced ourselves in a corner of the Grill Room, "What's your opinion of the Queen?"

"Needs more sex," Sybil said.

I choked on a sip of iced tea and spent a minute coughing and laughing into my napkin. Sybil beamed at me. "Well, she does!" she said, joining in my laughter. "Just look at the poor woman!"

I finally calmed down.

"Besides," Sybil said between bites, looking across the table at me with narrowed and calculating eyes, "Don't change the subject. I want to know why it is you wished to throttle the lovely Miss Warren a few minutes ago. Lord knows the creature deserves it."

"Would you believe a lover's spat?" I tried.

"Dear me, I don't think so," she responded smartly. "Without the benefit of a peek inside your boxers, I suspect you don't have the correct parts to appeal to that one."

"Ah," I said. Brillliant, witty repartee, that.

"No, you'll have to try again Mister Hacker," she said. "I must warn you, the gossip about you is deliciously wicked."

"Gossip?" I said. "Someone is gossiping about me? What, pray, are they saying?"

She paused while she attacked her plate with some gusto. She gazed at me while she ate, sizing me up. I did the same back at her. She was not All-American pretty, but she was an attractive woman. Instead of the perfect cheerleader features – a pert nose, the perfect cheekbones – Sybil; Montgomery's classic English features – long face and smallish chin – were offset by a lovely, creamy complexion and very pretty eyes. She looked intelligent and interesting and somewhat intriguing ... three descriptions that cannot usually be ascribed to the models on the cover of Vogue. But I liked her frank and forthright way.

"The gossip says you have managed to alienate our fuhrer," She said finally. "And it is known to be dangerous to clash wills with Big Wyn. The gossip further says that Big Wyn is trying to have you thrown the hell out of here."

"Well, even Big Wyn can't do that," I said. "We have something here in the Colonies called the First Amendment."

"But she can make life unpleasant," Sybil said. "And Julie Warren is often used for unpleasantness-making."

"Is she often used for physical assault?"

"How's that?" Sybil asked. I told her about the attack on Honie the previous evening and my suspicions about the identity of her assailant. Sybil's face darkened with concern and shock.

"Dear me," she said. "That does go beyond the pale. How is the poor girl?"

I told her Honie was recuperating. I took a sip of tea and looked out the window, gathering my thoughts.

"Look," I said. "What the hell gives here? What kind of operation is this? Wynnona Stilwell can have someone beat up and all you can say is that it's 'beyond the pale?' This is supposed to be a professional golf tour, not a Central American banana republic. You're not supposed to be able to have people you don't like rubbed out. What's going on?"

She reached over and patted my hand. "Now, now...calm down m'dear," she cooed. "You've got to understand that Wynnona Stilwell is one of those people who wear power like a suit of clothes. It is what she lives for, and she is very, very good at it. She has amassed a great deal of it running this Tour and she can expend it as she wishes."

"But—" I started to protest. Sybil held up her hand to silence me.

"She worked very hard to gain control of the sponsors and their money," she explained. "She controls who they are, what they pay and what they get in return, which is virtually anything they want. Because she's controlling the money, she has weight. She is able to control which players get certain endorsement deals, corporate outings and all kinds of other little sweetmeats. She controls who gets nice hotel rooms and free courtesy cars. She determines who gets interviewed by the media. If you are her friend, you get lots of perks that make one's life easier. If you're not her friend, life on Tour can be an unholy grind."

"So everyone sells out for the money," I said sadly.

"No, not necessarily," Sybil corrected me. "She has and uses other methods to gain control of some of the girls. Some not-so-nice ways, in fact."

I thought about the Carol Acorn episode. "You mean sexual."

Sybil nodded. "Keeping your sexuality hidden is one of the first rules on the Tour," she said. "We're supposed to be athletes, not women. The sponsors would like us all to be hetero and married, so they can get away with making sexist and leering comments. The Tour would like to pretend that none of us have sex with anyone, male or female. Yet at the same time, they have hired beauty consultants to come out on Tour and give us makeup lessons and other tips to make us more…presentable, I think was the word."

"They want you to be sexy looking, but not sexual," I said.

"Exactly," she nodded approvingly. "And it's a hetero-sexual model of sexiness that they promote. The beauty consultant was talking all about softness and femininity."

"I'll bet Julie Warren was taking lots of notes," I said.

She trilled her laughter, high and delicate.

"Anyway, that brand of heterosexual bias means that a lot of girls are running as fast as they can to get into the closet and stay there," Sybil said. "It's sad sometimes. I've know girls who tell their partners not to follow them around the golf course because it might not 'look right.' Can you imagine such a thing?"

She paused to eat some more. "Wynnona Stilwell, I think, knows all about that, and knows which ones she can exploit," she concluded. "And she does it without the slightest hesitation because of the power it gives her."

"But what about good old Harold?" I wondered. "What role does he have?"

"Perfect cover," Sybil laughed. "He spends his time fishing or fixing engines, but he's the official husband who can be trotted out whenever Wynnona needs an escort or the appearance of normalcy."

"She's sick," I said.

"Oh, absolutely," Sybil nodded as she munched on a carrot stick.

"So why is everyone putting up with it? What isn't someone raising the roof? Why are *you* putting up with it?"

"I don't have to put up with anything," she replied, staring at me. "I play about twenty weeks a year over here, win as much money as I can, and go back home. All my endorsement contracts and business associates are European. Wynnona cannot touch me and in fact she needs me and the other European girls to add some flash and allure to her Tour. So she ignores me completely, except when she needs something from me, and then she asks for it politely. I expect, and get, nothing else. And that's fine with me. More than fine, if you really want to know."

"And the others?" I pressed. "The young girls who step into this and get manipulated, assaulted or sexually abused? What about them?"

Sybil let the question hang in the air for a moment, then looked away. I thought I saw something like guilt cross her face like a brief shadow, but I wasn't sure.

"It's not my problem, is it then?" she said, finally.

I said nothing. But a wave of sadness washed over me. Sybil looked at me for a moment, then checked her watch and announced her need to go work on her putting. She got up and left.

I don't know how long I sat there, staring out the window, lost in thought. But when I finally got up to leave, the Grill Room was empty.

FIFTEEN

When I was a boy, maybe five or six years old, some men from the public works department came to our street to do some work on the sewer lines that ran underneath our street. I wandered out to watch, attracted by the noisy equipment and the flashing lights and the brawny men in their sweat-stained wife-beater undershirts. I remember the big yellow truck, the sawhorses set up on either side of the manhole cover to keep drivers away, and the big, ferocious, red-headed Irishman who drove the truck. He looked Bunyonesque.

It was that guy, muscles bulging, who had grabbed a metal bar with a hook on one end, insterted it into the cast-iron manhole cover and yanked the thing off with a mighty grunt. It flipped over with a loud metallic clank on the asphalt. Suddenly, the street was alive with dozens of rapidly scurrying cockroaches – big, hairy, two-inch-long bugs – awakened from a midday nap on their cozy and cool manhole lid and rudely thrust into the bright light of the afternoon sun. It had seemed to me at that moment that my big, hairy-chested truck driver friend had yanked the cover off the gates of hell and these hideous black demons were running around looking for lost souls to suck or tiny boys to carry back into that yawning black hole in the middle of my street.

I had run screaming back into my house while the city boys howled with laughter. The memory of that scene gave me nightmares for years.

It occurred to me that everything I had learned about the LPGA in the last seventy-two hours closely resembled that awful childhood afternoon. Almost against my will, the façade had been jerked back to reveal a scurrying, buggy rot underneath. I had long known of Big Wyn's reputation as a difficult woman. And nobody with any sense could possibly be shocked by the fact that there were lesbians playing on the Tour. Hell, there were probably some gay guys playing on the PGA Tour as well. So what?

But the "so what" was worse than that. Big Wyn was not just a difficult woman, but a manipulative one as well. And, perhaps, evil. Certainly, I had learned that she was not above, or beneath, using any tool to advance her already significant power. She seemed to be cruising through life, unconcerned about those she left behind in her wake, emotionally trashed or physically assaulted.

But why was I getting all upset? Like Sybil Montgomery said, it really wasn't my problem, was it? Who had appointed me the keeper of the universal flame of truth, justice and the American way? Had anyone else – especially one of the people more directly involved – jumped aboard that noble white steed and ridden off to do battle with the dragon that was Big Wyn? No. So why should some mild-mannered golf reporter named Hacker get his BVDs in a wad? My job was just to write pithy summaries of games, and perhaps some insightful summaries of why someone won. That's it. My job was not to rip the cover off the LPGA, nor to avenge the emotional damage done to someone like Carol Acorn, or the physical damage done to someone like Honie Carlton.

Unfortunately, my little self-directed talking-to didn't work. I did care. And I knew that someone needed to take a running tilt at this particular windmill. Dammit, there are some windmills that need tilting at, and this was one of them.

I went back to my hotel room and stood at the window for a long time, looking out at nothing and thinking deep thoughts. My reporter's instincts began to click and whir and grind into action. A plan began to take shape. I realized that I was operating with lots of rumor, innuendo, conjecture and the occasional bit of gossip. What I needed, I realized, were some hard facts and a little corroboration.

Something in my head whirred and clicked an idea into place. Aha! An idea!

I went to the telephone and started tracking down Danny Bell. Danny had been one of the many old newspaper friends who had "gone on to bigger and better things," as we like to say. Working for a newspaper is never a get-rich proposition. One does it because one loves it. Because it makes you get out of bed in the morning and go to work. Because you love the professional cynics with whom you work. Because you love the quick pace, the ever-changing conditions, and the feeling of accomplishment when you see your own words in print. Because you love the game of it, the sticking of well-deserved pins in the inflated egos of some parts of society, and the revealing of secrets that others would rather leave untold. Because you know that in some small way, you have been part of a larger enterprise, something called the search for truth.

But you don't do it because of the money. Because, God knows, the money is crap. And not everyone can get past that part of it. Danny Bell had loved being a newspaperman, but he needed more, He had a wife and kids. There are thousands of people like Danny who do it for a while, have a ball, and then "go on to other things." Higher-paying jobs, more responsibilities, the "real world."

Danny had gone to Detroit, tripled his salary when he began work for one of Detroit's auto giants. He had switched over to something called "public affairs." He wrote a little, attended lots of meetings, took people out to lunch, traveled some. He got paid big bucks for keeping his head down and staying out of trouble. That was the real world. But I needed him now, and after passing through several layers of operators, receptionists and secretaries, I finally got him on the telephone.

"Hacker my man!" he exclaimed. "How they hangin'?"

"Fine, Danny, fine" I assured him. "Keeping busy?"

"I've got a hellacious afternoon schedule," he said. "I got one call to make and one memo to write. I tell you, it's tough to come up with creative ways to keep from falling dead-ass asleep after lunch in this job!"

I laughed and asked about his wife and kids. In Boston, the Bell family had crammed itself into a tiny two-bedroom flat in Brookline. Now, they owned a spacious home in a nice Detroit suburb. Good schools for the kids, lots of friends and neighbors for the wife, probably belonged to a country club. The good life. It all likely made it worthwhile, in Danny's mind, his having to abide all the bullshit. Probably.

"So to what can I attribute the pleasure of this call?" Danny asked.

"God, you're starting to sound like someone in public affairs," I chided him. "I need some background for a piece I'm doing on the LPGA. I know your company used to be a major sponsor of the tournament up there. What do you know about it?"

He blew out his breath in a rush. "The LPGA?" he mused, "Yeah, I remember something about that. I wasn't directly involved in that program…it was more marketing's game than mine. You'd probably get better information out of the marketing veep. He was in the day-to-day trenches."

"Haven't got the time," I said. "Besides, I'm not so much looking for facts and figures as I am impressions. How they do business. Deep background stuff. You can be my anonymous but highly placed source."

"Whoopee," Danny said. "Make my friggin day! Okay, let me think. We sponsored the Ladies Michigan Open for what, about five years, I think. Research boys thought it was a good thing to put money into…they said that most major purchasing decisions, such as buying an automobile, are heavily influenced by women. And that sponsoring a women's sporting event would help us, ummm, access that buying demographic. That's how those weenies talk. Impressions per million eye parts and crap like that."

I made a gagging sound in my throat.

"Yeah, me too," Danny said. "But sometimes they're right."

"I always thought men bought the cars," I said.

"Me, too," he said. "But the research shows that as much as we like to think we're making the decision after looking under the hood, kicking the tires and listening to the sound of a car door shutting, it's the wife who says yea or nay. Same with most major purchase decisions."

"So did it work?" I asked.

"Tournament sponsorship? Nah, not really. First of all, there wasn't national TV coverage until the last year, and then only on cable. So that limited our exposure to all those eye parts pretty drastically. Even the sports writers like you refused to use our name in the stories about the tournament … it was always the 'Ladies Michigan Open.' Like we didn't even exist. Didn't do us diddly-squat in terms of selling cars, you ask me. I think the whole thing was basically an excuse for our publicity-mad president to have an excuse to go out and play golf and get photographed with glamorous women golfers."

"Are there any?" I asked. Danny laughed. "So you didn't renew the contract?"

"As I recall, there were some serious negotiations with the LPGA when it came time to renew," he said. "And I seem to remember that one of the main reasons we decided to bail out was a whole series of heavy demands the tour laid on us."

"Such as …?"

"Ummm, this is the deep background part, and it's been a few years now, so don't hold me to any high standards of accuracy, but I think they wanted a fleet of our top-line cars for the top brass and best players to use while they were in town. And some major new bucks to become one of the entire LPGA's top sponsors. And ... according to rumors that filtered up through the gossip grapevine ... there was something about an under-the-table demand for some appearance money for some of the bigger names."

"Appearance money?" I was surprised. "Nobody gets appearance money in this country. That only happens in Asia and sometimes in Europe. It's downright un-American, like blackmail or something."

"Yeah, something like that," Danny said. "The number I heard was a cool hundred grand for each of five players, tax-free and silent. Our legal beagles about shit their pants when they heard about it. Said the IRS woulda clamped down so hard everyone's dick woulda fallen off."

"Did you ever hear who was supposed to get the cash?" I wondered.

"Not officially," Danny said. "But one of the guys involved in the negotiations told me in the men's room one afternoon that the LPGA had asked for a lump-sum payment and that the head honcho over there would parcel it out."

"Who was that?"

"That big broad...what's her name? Stilwell...Wynnona Stilwell. She was handling all the negotiations. Balls of brass, that one," Danny laughed. "She was going to parcel the cash out to the best five players as an extra incentive to come to Michigan to play. Then she wanted us to lean on the network to make sure they got plenty of air time as well. Did you ever? Our people took great pleasure in telling her to go jump, let me tell you."

"Very interesting," I said. "I wonder if other sponsors got the same kind of ... er...opportunity to invest in the LPGA?"

"Oh, hell, I imagine so," Danny said. "Stuff like that is rampant in this day and age. You wouldn't believe what our sponsorship deal in fooball covers. Booze...bimbos...skybox seats...weekends in Vegas. The accountants and the lawyers figure out how much they can disguise as legitimate business expense, and the marketing guys use it to entertain people. Be a pretty good story if you wanted to rip the cover off that can of worms," he said.

"You want to be the source?" I asked.

"And get fired and probably sent to jail?" he said drily. "I think not."

"OK, I'll stick with golf," I said.

"Yeah, you and our fearless leader," Danny said. He was referring to his company's celebrity-like CEO who had turned the company around from loss to profit and made himself famous along the way by starring in most of the company's TV commercials. "Playing in pro-ams was one of his favorite things," Danny continued, "And many of us suspected it was the only reason why we invested in the LPGA sponsorship. But, now that I'm thinking about that whole scene, I seem to recall that the last year, he came away ticked off because his pro wouldn't talk to him the entire round. He came back and said he'd never met such a bitch in his entire life. You know, come to think of it, it was that Stilwell woman he was playing with that year. Huh! Never thought of that before, It fits, though."

"Yeah," I said. "She has a reputation for being difficult at times."

"Well," Danny said, "Difficult is one thing. Pissing off a major sponsor and losing funding from a corporation with pretty deep pockets is something else. Stupid, I'd say."

I thanked Danny for the information and promised to call him next time I was in Detroit. The shadows of the afternoon had given way to the curtain of dusk. I began to think about dinner, where and with whom. As if in answer, there was a knock at my door.

I opened it to find Sybil Montgomery standing there, smiling at me brightly. Her hair was brushed back from her face which carried the sheen of newly applied makeup. She had a big bottle of champagne in one hand and two crystal glasses in the other.

"I believe the sun has officially descended over the yard-arm," she pronounced.

"And?" I blocked the door, keeping her standing out in the hall.

"And I thought we should get together and celebrate the end of a nice day and having met one another."

"And?"

"And I thought it important to prove to you that not all female professional golfers are ... er ... anti-man."

"Well," I said. "Since this is a scientific inquiry, please come in." I stepped out of the way and bowed her into my room.

Later, after room service had brought dinner, after we had polished off the champagne, and after we had talked and talked, sitting together out on the tiny patio that was barely wide enough to sit on without scraping knees ... after we had watched the twilight deepen from shades of pink and orange into blues and purples and finally into black...after we had listened to the city sounds dwindle and fade and give way to the night sounds of insects and birds and the soft rustling of the palms on the evening breeze ... after I had reached out to hold her slender but strong hand in mine in the quiet of the evening, sharing the feeling of connection with the cosmos around us ...

After all of that, we rose as one and went inside. And performed the next part of our scientific experiment. We shed our clothes silently in the cool darkness of the room leaving the door to the patio open, so that the sounds of the night could come inside with us. We were silent as we explored each other's body, luminescent in the near darkness, passing hands softly into those firery secret places, reveling in the tactile sensations that were heightened by the soft caress of the cool air flowing gently into the room.

And then we added our own sounds to the night world as we began our rhythmic pleasures. Slowly, oh so slowly, then faster and faster, our bodies moved together and our breaths, intermingled, came faster. Soft stolen cries rent the air. Until we both reached the final exhalation, the gentle death, and we sank slowly and gratefully back to earth together, joined, warmed, deepened, released, sated.

It was, for me, a necessary thing. A reaffirmation of the good that is in life. A reminder that all of creation is not bad or evil or wicked. I felt, in those moments before sleep overtook me, reconnected with humanity, with pleasure, with fun. I slept, I am sure, with a smile on my face.

SIXTEEN

I woke early and alone. I sat up and scanned the room, which appeared empty. I couldn't see any sign of the activities of the previous evening. No champagne bottles left overturned. No lipstick-smeared glasses. No tidbits of underwear scattered about. No hurriedly scribbled notes on my pillow: "Thanks for a good time, ya big lug!" It was if nothing had happened, which led me to wonder if anything really had happened.

Sighing, I went to the bathroom. No lipstick hearts drawn on the mirror. Empty.

"*Tis brief, m'lord. As woman's love.*"

I got on this Shakespeare kick in college, in between golf tournaments, and I used to know whole scenes by rote. Don't ask me why. It's a skill that doesn't come in particularly handy either playing or writing about golf. But odd bits and pieces come flooding back to me at the strangest times, and one of the oddest is after sex. Like this morning, in the shower, those two lines. *Hamlet* always was such a buzz kill anyway.

It was regret, I figured. Not over the act itself, but for the briefness of the glow it had produced. There was never enough glow and it never lasted long enough.

I shrugged it off in the steam of the shower and made ready to face the world anew. It was another golden Florida morning, it was Friday, and the golf tournament was underway. The LPGA, unlike the male counterpart, usually stages three-round tournaments. But the fact that golf was being played outside was reason enough to gird the loins and head forth.

The telephone interrupted me in mid-gird.

"Hacker?" said a soft voice on the other end, It was Honie Carlton. I slapped my forehead in sudden anguish. My episode with Sybil has pushed all thought of my injured and hospital-bound young friend out of my head. I was immediately and intensely guilty.

"Honie!" I started to babble. "How are you feeling? Where are you? Are you okay? ..."

She stopped my rush of words with a tiny laugh.

"Oh, Hacker, shut up and listen," she said. There was a tiny reminder of the pre-attack lilt in her voice. "I'm fine. I'm back at the hotel. My boss flew in from Texas last night and is taking care of things. Now listen, I just heard some big news! You won't believe it! Benton Bergmeister is dead!"

I was, as they say, struck dumb. Bergmeister had also faded out of my consciousness that night we had come upon

Honie after her attack. In the excitement of getting her to the hospital, I had forgotten about old Benton. And that he had been about to tell me why he was quitting the LPGA Tour. I guess he really had. Quit, that is.

"Hacker? Are you there?" Honie demanded petulantly. "Did you hear what I just said?"

"I heard, I heard," I said. "When, where and how?"

"I don't know," she said. "I just overheard Karla — she's my boss — talking to someone. She ran out of here all afluster, so they must have just found out."

"Thanks, kid," I said. "I'm on the case. Anything you need?"

"Naw," she said. "Go get 'em."

I got. In the lobby, there was no outward manifestation of anything abnormal going on. People were coming out of elevators, heading for the restaurant buffet, sitting in chairs reading the morning papers, and booking tours with the concierge. Just a typical day, modern American resort-style.

Behind the front desk, the hotel staffers were also going about their business, cashing guests out and snapping for bellmen. Except for one youngish girl with pretty blond hair, who was standing over to one side, almost out of sight. Her face had gone pure white and she held a hand over her mouth in the traditional pose of shock. I watched as an older man in a gray suit wandered past her, stopping to whisper something urgently in her ear. She immediately shook her head as if to clear out the cobwebs, and jumped back to work, picking up a stack of papers and heading for the nearest computer terminal.

But that told me that something unusual was afoot.

I made a beeline for the security trailer hidden in its little grove of bushes. When I walked in, Don Collier was talking on the phone. He hung up as soon as he saw me.

"Hiya, Don," I said pleasantly. "Where's the stiff?"

He stared at me. "What? Who? How? He started three different questions, almost simultaneously.

I laughed. "Word travels fast," I said. Especially amongst us newshounds. So what's the scoop?"

He sighed deeply. One of the telephones on his desk began an insistent chirping. He flipped it a bird and jumped up from his chair. "Fuck it," he growled. "I'm tired of talking with the suits and PR types. C'mon, you might as well walk with me. You seem to know everything anyway."

He led me back into the hotel, to the north wing, to the third floor. Benton Bergmeister had been assigned an "inside room," which was a euphemistic way of saying he had a room with a parking lot view. Oh, away in the distance one could catch a glimpse of the Olympic-size outdoor pool, but it still was a parking-lot view. Big Wyn enjoyed the palatial suite with views across the golf course, while the poor commish, who had the misfortune of possessing a dick, got the parking lot.

There were about a half-dozen plainclothes cops in Benton's room, all of whom seemed to be doing something officious. All of whom were totally ignoring the body of Benton Bergmeister lying in his bed, naked, pale and sagging. He lay on his back, one arm by his side, the other flung casually across his pale and flaccid belly. He looked, as do most dead people, smaller and somewhat shrunken. His eyes were closed, his mouth slightly ajar, as if he had died in midsnore. In fact, he looked like he was still asleep. Which I guess he was, in a nap that would last forever.

The room was neat and clean. Bergmeister's briefcase lay on the desk, open, with papers spilling out onto the desktop. Next to the briefcase was a bottle of Scotch, empty save for about two inches in the bottom. There were no clothes scattered about, which struck me as odd since Benton was undeniably naked. I guess he was a neat stiff.

One of the cops saw us and walked over. He nodded at Collier. "Hey Don," he said. "We're about done here. Who's this?"

"Hacker," Collier answered. The cop looked at me with flat, penetrating, clear gray eyes. "He's a reporter. Doing a story on the women's tour."

"Guess he's got something to write about," the cop said. He nodded over at Benton's body.

"What happened?" I asked.

"Guy died," the cop said and walked away.

"Friendly people here in Miami," I said loudly to Collier. "I thought all the asshole cops worked in Boston."

The cop spun on his heel at that, but Collier hustled me out of the room.

"Cause of death?" I asked.

"They're not sure," Collier told me. "Hopefully, it's a heart attack or stroke or something natural."

"Yeah, that'd get the monkey off the hotel's back," I agreed.

"Cynical, but true," Collier nodded. "It might also be suicide. In addition to the booze, there were a whole lot of prescription bottles in the guy's bathroom, and several of them were empty or nearly so. One of the dicks said that if he had mixed some of those pills with the booze, it woulda been a no-no. Quiet but effective way to check out."

"Inconvenient," I said. "But again, not the hotel's fault. People check in to check out all the time, right?" Collier nodded. "Of course, maybe somebody offed poor old Benton."

"Shit, Hacker," the hotel man bristled. "Don't even think that! You saw that room. There wasn't the first hint of foul play in there. Guy took off his clothes, hung them up, laid down to sleep and didn't wake up. One way or another."

The smart-ass cop came out into the hallway and lit a cigarette. He blew out the smoke silently while he fixed those steady gray eyes on Collier and me.

"M.E. on the way?" Collier asked. The cop nodded. His eyes never moved. "Well, let me know what he says. I got an entire front office ready to shit themselves. Not good on the publicity front, you know what I mean."

The cop shrugged. I could tell he wasn't going to stay up nights worrying about the problems the executives of the Doral Hotel and Country Club were having on the publicity front.

"Listen," I said to the cop before we left. "I don't know if it means anything or not, but a couple of nights ago, Bergmeister told me that he was planning to quit his job."

The cop's right eyebrow ticked upwards a centimeter or two. I could tell he was drooling with interest. "That so?" he said, letting more smoke drift out of his nose.

"Yeah," I said. "And my impression was that he was damn glad to be getting out of here. I think he was tired of working for a bunch of women."

"I can understand that," the cop said as he turned to go back into the room. "Workin' for women will fuckin' kill ya."

SEVENTEEN

Collier promised to let me know what the medical examiner had to say about the cause of Benton Bergmeister's death. So I headed for the tournament pressroom, where about ten fellow members of the Fourth Estate had gathered to report on the first round of the tournament, just getting underway.

I could see where Honie had her work cut out for her. On a typical first-round day on the PGA Tour, there would be at least thirty reporters, writers and photographers hanging around, looking for stories. By the weekend, that number would triple, depending on the size of the city. Now, Miami is a pretty big media market, but only ten sportswriters had stirred themselves to attend the big doings of the LPGA visit to their town. Actually, only eight. The two guys

I knew in the pressroom were Barley Raney from the AP and Penny Schoenfeld, a stringer for *Golf World* magazine.

Barley is an old and happy drunk. Short and heavy-set, his face is a riot of capillary explosions, as though someone had taken his face and shoved it against a plate-glass window a hundred times in a row. His heyday as a golf writer had been back in the Sixties: He had covered the ascension of "King Jack" and the Fall of the House of Palmer. Now, although well past retirement age, Barley was still hanging on. He had no doubt volunteered to cover the LPGA for AP, which allowed him to continue to follow the sun around the country, pounding out his thirty graphs a week, plus notes. Whether or not any of the AP's subscribers actually used his stuff was beside the point – he was doing the only thing in life he knew how to do.

Penny covered maybe a dozen women's events for the magazine. I think she was married to someone rich and worked not so much for the money, which was bad, but for the chance to get out of the house on occasion. She wasn't a bad writer, but she rarely, if ever, left the air-conditioned comfort of the press room. I remember watching her play golf once, down in Myrtle Beach, and I don't ever want to see that again.

The rest of the "crowd" were the locals—some TV and some print. They sat around waiting for something to happen, and on the first day of a tournament, that can be a long wait. Out on the course, the early tee times featured the Tour's younger and not-yet-famous players. Later tee times were heavily seeded with the tour's better players, since the fans usually don't come out in any numbers until after lunch.

Sitting in the front of the press room, a telephone glued to her ear, was an attractive woman, mid-forties, wearing a nice blue dress with a fashionable scarf affixed jauntily on one shoulder, a string of pearls and some dangly earrings. I guessed her to be Karla, Honie's boss, fresh in from Texas.

"Say!" I yelled loudly toward the front of the room and at no one in particular. "Are you going to have a press conference or just release an official statement about Benton Bergmeister?"

I watched as the lady in the blue dress looked up in surprise, murmured something into her telephone and hung up.

One of the TV guys – he wore a very nice tan – looked over at me.

"Who's this Bergmisher?"

"Bergmeister," I corrected him. "He's the commissioner of the LPGA Tour. Or was, I guess, since he just croaked. The cops are crawling all over his room upstairs right now."

"No shit?" the TV guy yelled. Nothing like breaking news to crease the follicles of the blow-dried set. He leaped to the nearest phone and began to frantically dial. The other reporters woke up en masse and began firing questions at Karla. I just smiled. Hacker kicks over beehive and watches chaos ensue. It's a role I am most justly famous for, if I do say so myself.

"Hold on, hold on," Karla in blue was saying, trying to get control of the situation. "I'm not hiding anything. I was about to make an announcement, but I was just waiting for the go-ahead from the police first."

"Bullcrap, lady," Barley yelled at her in his ear-piercing basso profundo. "You was holdin' out on us. Now give!"

Karla sighed. "All I can tell you is that Benton Bergmeister, the commissioner of the LPGA Tour, was found dead in his room this morning. The police are investigating and the Dade County Medical Examiner will be releasing information later today concerning the cause of death."

"Was there foul play involved?" Penny Schoenfeld asked.

Karla blanched and shook her head. "No, Penny, we don't have any indication of that at this time. But that's why I wanted to wait until ..."

"Do you think that the fact that Benton Bergmeister was about to announce his resignation as commissioner had any bearing on his death?" I shouted out. Giving the beehive yet another well-placed kick.

Karla rocked back as if someone had just slapped her. But, being the true public relations professional, she quickly recovered her composure. "I don't know where you got that information," she said coldly, "But I suggest you double-check it. Sounds like a rumor to me."

Slick, I thought. She dodged the question without answering it straight out. Trouble was, ole Barley Raney had spent a lifetime working around slick PR types, and he, too, noted the evasion.

"C'mon, lady," he growled, "It's getting hip-deep in here. Was Bergy 'in' or 'out?' Guy was always fun to drink with," he added in a typical Barley nonsequitur.

Karla paused a moment before she answered this time. Another good PR move – make sure you can control the answers. "Benton Bergmeister was scheduled to retire in two years," she said carefully, throwing me a glare. "That's when he would have reached the mandatory retirement age set by the LPGA's policy board. There had been some discussions between the board and Benton concerning early retirement, but as far as I know, no final decisions had been reached."

Barley looked over at me and threw me a wink. "He was out," he growled, and reached for his phone.

"Now, hold on," Karla said, looking worried all of a sudden. "I have to insist that you act responsibly in this matter and not resort to printing half-truths or rumors without verification. I would hope that as professional journalists, you would await the facts in this matter and not ..."

"Professional journalists, my ass," boomed a voice from the back of the room. "They ain't nothin' but a bunch of stiffs and rewrite men, the lot of 'em!"

We all turned to see Big Wyn Stilwell making her way up to the interview stage at the front of the room. She was dressed in her golf outfit, a loud, pink-check thing.

"Hey Wyn," Barley boomed at her. "You got something about ole Benton?"

"Well, yes, Barley, as a matter of fact, I do," she said, settling into a chair and picking up the microphone as if she was to the stage born. Karla, the PR lady, showed immense relief at having a higher authority take command of the damage control. When the boss is present and talking, there's no longer any need to cover one's own ass, so Karla stepped back into the shadows and let Big Wyn take over.

"I have had the pleasure of knowing and working with Benton for the last five years," Wyn started. Her face had become serious and earnest. "I was shocked to hear this morning of his passing, and I know all the players share my sense of dismay and grief. Benton Bergmeister did great work for the LPGA, and his time and talents will be sorely missed by us all."

It was a perfect speech, hitting all the right notes. It was both bravura and bull. The press lemmings were writing down every word she said. It was time for another kick to the beehive.

"Is it true that Benton had discussed his resignation with you two days ago?" I asked.

Big Wyn glanced in my direction. She smiled, but her eyes were cold and hard.

"Absolutely not," she said grimly.

"Was he troubled by the state of management of the Tour, specifically the high degree of day-to-day control over the business affairs of the Tour by the Player's Council," I pressed. Out of the corner of my eye, I saw Barley snap to attention. I'm sure he had never heard a question like that tossed at Big Wyn Stilwell.

A couple of dangerous-looking red spots appeared high on Big Wyn's cheekbones. But, to her credit, she kept her anger bottled up.

"Benton had never said anything of that kind directly to me," Wynnona said slowly. "I guess you'll have to ask the other members of the council if he expressed concerns to them."

"So to your knowledge," I asked, "Bergmeister was not upset about his job and his continued usefulness and was not on the verge of walking out?"

"No," Big Wyn answered. But her eyes narrowed as she suddenly understood what I was doing. I knew she would deny all hints of trouble in the hen house. But by asking them in public, I was putting a bug in the ears of my fellow reporters. Benton Bergmeister's death was a news event, for sure, but not an especially significant one. But, on the other hand, if there was some internal squabbling going on about the Tour's management, well, that was a pretty good story. And it put Big Wyn right in the headlights.

She knew this, instinctively, and knew she had to do something about it. Quick.

"Benton's health had not been the best in the last few months," she said now. "He and I had talked some weeks ago about the possibility of his taking early retirement if he didn't start to feel better. I told Benton that of course we needed his services, but that his first responsibility was to himself, his family and his health, and that we would understand if he felt he was jeopardizing any of that by continuing to serve as our commissioner. After we had that chat, he had been feeling much better, so the subject was never brought up again. We all thought he was in good shape heading into the summer, but ..."

She left that thought dangling. Poor Benton. The Grim Reaper had come calling unexpectedly. What a shame.

"Does he have a family?" I asked.

Big Wyn's head came up and she looked at me. This time I saw, for a fleeting instant, a predator's glint in her eyes. It was that glint of victory when the kill has been completed and the prey lies in the grass, bleeding from wounds of throat and viscera, eyes open but unseeing, waiting to be devoured. It was just a fraction of a second, that look, but I caught it and in those nanoseconds I heard the plaintive howling across the grassy plains, the primitive beating of the breast, the thump of the drums in the background announcing the victory.

"He was married once," she told us. "But divorced some years ago. I believe he had a daughter."

That was all she said. But the remembrance of that look sent chills racing up and down my spine.

EIGHTEEN

Less than an hour later, we had a mimeographed obituary of Benton Bergmeister in hand, thanks to the efficient LPGA staff. The summary of his life did not mention his heavy drinking, nor his stated intention to resign. We had all been busy filing stories on the man's demise and what it would mean to the Tour, long- and short-term. I put in a paragraph in my story questioning the appropriateness of the Tour continuing to stage its tournament despite the death of its commissioner, but I knew my balls-less editor would take it out. He understands that a simple death of a relative nonentity will never get in the way of American sporting commerce. I mean, they didn't even hold off the NFL two days after JFK's assassination. Everyone understood that the LPGA would soldier on.

Before breaking for lunch, I decided to head out to the practice range and get some reaction quotes from some of the famous players. My route took me through the main lobby of the hotel, where I ran into Honie Carlton. She was wearing a turban-style head bandage from her attack the night before and she was chatting with an elderly lady who was improbably wearing a light cardigan sweater draped over her shoulders. It was probably ninety-two outside in the sun.

"Hacker!" Honie called to me when she saw me. I trudged over dutifully. "Hacker, this is Ethel Burbank," Honie introduced the old woman. "She is, or was, Benton's secretary back at headquarters."

I studied the woman. She was well into her sixties, with wispy, silvery hair pushed back from her face. Horn-rimmed spectacles hung on a string around her neck, where they banged into her formidable bosom as she moved. She was quite obviously distraught. She was clutching a damp-looking tissue in one hand and her face was red with splotches.

"How do you do?" I said politely. "I am sorry about your boss."

"Yes, yes, it's terrible, isn't it?" she said breathlessly. "I just heard about it as I was finishing my breakfast! What a dear, dear man he was."

"Ethel has worked for Benton for more than ten years," Honie explained to me. "They were a real team."

"Oh, that poor man," Ethel began weeping, dabbing at her eyes with her tissue. Honie wrapped her arms around the older woman and hugged her. Over Ethel's shoulder, she gave me an eye-rolling look.

"Mrs. Burbank," I said gently. The two women separated. "When did you last speak to Benton?"

"Well, now, let me see," Ethel said, mostly to herself. But I did note a return of sharpness to her eyes. Ethel Burbank was nobody's fool. "I spoke to him several times yesterday," she mused. "We always conversed first thing in the morning. Took care of the usual detail work at that time. Correspondence, telephone messages, things like that. But he called me later that morning and asked me to fly right down to Miami. He said he needed my help today in preparing something."

"Do you often join him out on Tour?" I asked.

"Very rarely, dear," she said, nodding. "I really have enough to do back at the office. But Benton said this was important, and that he needed me to fly right down. So I did."

"Did he say what it was he needed?"

"He didn't give me any details, dearie," Ethel said, dabbing at her welling eyes again. "I think...he said something about needing to prepare some materials for presentation to the players' council. But I don't know what he wanted. Frankly, I thought he might just be making the whole thing up to give me an excuse to come to Miami. He knew how much I loved going to the racetrack."

At that thought, she broke down again, her shoulders shaking. Honie, bless her nurturing heart, put her arms around the woman and cried with her. I stood there thinking while they wept, oblivious to the stares of curious passers-by in the lobby. After a minute or two, they were finished.

"Miz Burbank, may I ask you just one more question?" I began. Wiping her eyes with her now-drenched tissue, she nodded.

"Did anyone else here in Miami know you were coming? I mean, anyone from the LPGA?"

She fixed me with a level gaze, her eyes liquid but sharp. "Why no, dearie," she said. "I don't think so. Except for Miz Casey, of course. I called her to book me a flight and arrange a room. She's our travel expert you know."

Honie and I exchanged a glance. Then she grabbed Ethel by the arm and walked her off. I stood and watched them go.

Casey Carlyle, the Delicious One, Big Wyn's eyes and ears. She had known that Benton had asked his personal assistant to fly down to Miami suddenly. I had no doubt that Casey had pried the reason for Ethel's visit out of the old woman. So Casey, and soon Big Wyn, had known that Benton was preparing something to present to the player's council. Big Wyn had known something was up, despite her demurrals at this morning's press conference.

Had she confronted Benton and scared him to death? Not an outlandish assumption, after what I had learned about the woman over the last several days. Or had Benton's death been a coincidence, his alcohol-soaked body giving out at just the right time? For some reason, it was the latter scenario I found the most far fetched.

Out on the practice range, a dozen players were striking balls, preparing for the first round. Already, some twenty three-somes had teed off, from both the first and tenth tees. The afternoon wave was about to begin. Down at the far corner, I spotted Mary Beth Burke talking beside the water jug with Sybil Montgomery. I made a beeline.

"Afternoon, ladies," I said as I approached. "I need some suitably morose quotes about Benton Bergmeister for tomorrow's paper."

"Quit, Hacker," Mary Beth chastised me. "I thought he was a nice old guy. It's so sad."

"Right," I echoed. "'Nice guy. Real sad.' Sybil? Got anything to add to that?"

She stared back at me. "How did it happen, Hacker?" she wanted to know. "What killed the poor man?"

"Don't know yet," I told them. "There'll be an autopsy, probably this afternoon. For now, the police are assuming the guy just croaked."

I saw Mary Beth and Sybil exchange a glance. I couldn't read anything into it.

"It's just a bit too neat and clean for me," I said. "I mean, Benton told me a couple nights ago that he was thinking of quitting. I just found out that he called his secretary yesterday and had her fly in last night. She was supposed to help him prepare something to present to the player's council. Then, he dies. From what I had gathered from the man, he was feeling like singing about something Big Wyn did or didn't do to him. But now he's dead. Pretty convenient for Big Wyn, huh?"

The two women looked at each other again. Something was passing between the two. As a mere mortal man, I knew not what it was.

"So I'm thinking there's something below the surface going on," I concluded. "And from what I've learned about this organization in the last few days, it doesn't surprise me in the least that whatever's going on might be nasty and subterranean. And watching you guys giving each other the secret look tells me I'm right and that you know what it is."

They gave each other that look one more time, then looked at me. Perfectly blank-faced and innocent.

"I don't know what you're talking about," Burkey said calmly.

"Nor I," said my British friend.

"Oh, bull," I exploded. "We all are familiar with Big Wyn's way of working, and we all know she had some kind of grip on poor Benton's balls. He was about to break loose, finally, no matter how painful that might have been. But I don't know what that hold was, and you both do. So tell me, for God's sake."

They looked at each other one more time. Another secret message passed. They turned back to me.

"Well, Hacker," Burkey started, "We don't know exactly what Big Wyn had on Bergie. All we know is the rumor that's been around for years. Could be true, or it could be malicious gossip. That's up to you to decide."

"Okay," I nodded. "That's fair. What was it?"

Mary Beth sighed. "Well, the word was that Benton got caught in some kind of sexual fling with one of the rookies in his first year on the job. She was really a rookie, too, like about sixteen years old. That might have gotten Benton some jail time, if it were true. But the rumor is that Big Wyn bailed him out, had the whole episode buried and put Benton's balls in her pocketbook."

"Do you know who the young player was?" I asked. "Is she still playing today? Where does she live?"

I could smell the story now, and like a hunting dog, I was suddenly pitched into a fever of excitement. There were no fences too high, no thickets to overgrown, no holes too deep to prevent me from sniffing my way to the lair and howling to the sky at my discovery.

Burkey shook her head. "Nope," she said. "Neither of us ever heard a name to go with the story. Like I said, it could be there wasn't a real person involved. Could be the whole thing was someone's imagination all along."

"Guess I'll have to do some digging," I said. "Somebody's got to know something."

"Hold on, Hacker," Sybil cautioned. "You're leaping the hedgerow without your mount. I shouldn't think you'll have much luck running around here trying to get someone to help you dig up dirt about the Tour or about the late Mr. Bergmeister. We all liked him, you know. We players tend to band together whenever someone threatens our Tour. I think you'd best let Mary Beth and I muck about quietly and see if we can uncover the name of the unlucky lass in this alleged episode. Don't you agree, Mary Beth?"

"That's A-One correct," Mary Beth drawled. "If anybody does know something, they're more likely to confide some gossip to Sybil here or me instead of some wise-ass reporter who's a goddam Yankee to boot."

"Here, here," Sybil laughed. They stared at me, compatriots in secret messages and the sisterhood, and tried not laugh aloud. But the smiles playing at the edge of their lips gave them away.

"Damn, it's hard being a man," I said.

Their peals of laughter rang out over the range.

NINETEEN

I noticed a good sized gallery gathering around the first tee and strolled over to see who was about to begin her round. A young tournament volunteer held a sign on a pole that listed the members of the group about to tee off. Rosie Jones, a perennially tough competitor, was one of the three, along with Ellen Ferguson, a player I knew nothing about. The third name was Wynnona Stilwell.

I elbowed my way through the crowd to get next to the ropes. Rosie, dressed stylishly in Jamie Sadock threads, was standing on the tee box, staring down the fairway in rapt concentration. Ellen, a pretty, twenty-something with golden brown hair, stood nervously next to her caddie, swishing her driver back and forth, waiting to get started.

The tournament starter also seemed nervous, and kept glancing at his watch. The man wore a broad-brimmed

Panama hat against the Florida sun and a short-sleeved white shirt and necktie. He studied his clipboard, glanced again at his watch, and tried to peer over the heads of the assembled crowd. He was looking for Big Wyn, the third member of the group, who was nowhere to be found.

"Stilwell's not here," I heard someone in the crowd whisper. "It's almost one thirty-two. Where is she?"

"Could be a scratch," another fan whispered back. "But if she doesn't show up before the group is announced, she's disqualified."

The rumor of Big Wyn's possible disqualification swept through the gallery like wildfire. Rosie Jones ignored the hub-bub and continued to stare, focused, down the fairway, plan-ning her tee shot and the one after that. The other golfer heard the whispers in the crowd, and leaned over to say some-thing softly to her caddie. The two of them grinned, appar-ently not at all disappointed not to have to play this round with a living legend.

The starter looked at his watch one more time, shook his head sadly and picked up an electronic microphone to announce the players in the group. As if on cue, just at that last possible moment, there was a murmur and then the gal-lery parted like the Red Sea and a determined-looking Wynnona Stilwell marched onto the tee, followed by her cad-die. The gallery burst into loud applause and heaved what seemed to be a common sigh of relief.

It occurred to me, suddenly, that Big Wyn's last-second appearance had been contrived. It was a small psych game, waiting until the very last instant to appear on the tee. It let her opponents know that Big Wyn was the star, the alpha bitch whom everyone had come to watch, and the one golfer who could – and would – push the envelope to the limit and get away with it.

Big Wyn now strode around, shaking hands with officials and her opponents. I saw Ellen Ferguson's face blanch when Stilwell had walked onto the tee, but she bravely shook Big Wyn's proffered hand. Rosie Jones, on the other hand, never moved, blinked or otherwise acknowledged Big Wyn's presence. It was apparent that the long-time veteran had seen this act before and refused to play along.

"Ladies and gentlemen," the starter now intoned into his speaker. "The one thirty-two group. From Bolton, Vermont, in her second year on tour, please welcome Ellen Ferguson!" The gallery gave the girl a polite round of applause. "From Atlanta, in her fifteenth year on tour, Rosie Jones!" The applause was louder and lasted a few seconds longer. Rosie, who had been fishing something out of her golf bag, held up her hand in acknowledgement.

"And finally, a player who needs no introduction," the starter said, beginning to sound like the announcer at a prize fight, "From Phoenix, Arizona, the winner of 32 tournaments, including the U.S. Open and the U.S. Amateur, one of golf's living legends, Big Wyn Stilwell!"

The burst of noise split the humid air, a solid wall of sounds, accentuated by whistles and cheers, that lasted for more than three minutes. Big Wyn reveled in it. She removed her visor and waved it high above her head, and when the applause picked up noise and momentum, she threw her head back and laughed in delight. Big Wyn was in her element, basking in the adoration of her fans.

It was right about then that her glance fell on me, standing on the ropes. I was not cheering or clapping or whistling. I was standing there with my arms crossed, staring at her. I'm sure she read on my face what I was thinking, because her own countenance darkened and her eyes narrowed. For that moment, we were gladiators, facing off in the Coliseum; knights about to begin a joust; linemen on opposite sides of scrimmage at the Super Bowl.

The crowd finally fell silent. Big Wyn broke away from my stare. "Go ahead, honey," Big Wyn said loudly to the youngest member of the threesome. "Show us what you got."

The crowd chuckled, but Ferguson shot an angry glance at Big Wyn. She did not appreciate the condescending tone nor the bald attempt at psychological warfare. Her drive was a fine one, but it drifted in the wind a bit to the right and finished well down the fairway in the first cut of rough. She was rewarded with a fine round of applause. I watched her shoulders heave in relief. The first one is always the hardest.

Rosie Jones was next. Big Wyn knew better than to try a psych job on the veteran and kept silent. Jones methodically teed her ball, went through her pre-shot routine and launched a beautiful drive that split the fairway. The fans cheered.

Then, Big Wyn stepped forward. "C'mon Wyn," someone yelled. "Do it, Mama!" cried another.

Wyn teed her ball, then strode over to her caddie, selected her driver, and took a couple of practice swings. She was frozen at address, ready to pull the club back, when someone behind me snapped a picture of her. The distinctive, high-pitched whine of the camera's motor drive resounded like a gunshot in the abnormal silence of golf.

Big Wyn stepped away from her ball and looked over in my direction. I smiled at her.

"Goddam it," she snapped loudly at the tournament official standing nearby. "That son-of-a-bitch did that on purpose! I want his press credentials confiscated and his sorry ass thrown the hell out of here!"

Her outburst stunned the crowd into silence. The official, white-faced, strode over to the ropes where I stood. I continued smiling and held my hands out to show him. Empty.

"Tweren't me, Wyn," I said gaily. "Nice try, though."

Behind me, we all heard a quavering voice. "I-I-I'm sorry. I didn't realize ..." We all turned around to see a white-haired old dear, clutching her Kodak to her chest. She looked mortified.

"There are no cameras allowed on the course during the tournament," the official told the woman sternly. He turned to Big Wyn, who was still glaring angrily at me, shrugged in apology and held up his hand. "Quiet, please," he intoned.

Big Wyn slammed her driver on the turf in frustration. She threw one last glare my way before turning again to the task at hand. But I could tell her concentration wasn't on golf. She hurried now, made a jerky, rough pass at the ball, and hooked her shot into a fairway bunker waiting down the left side. A bad start, all around.

The gallery groaned in sympathy. "That's okay, Wyn," cried one supporter. "You can do it."

She looked at me again before striding off down the fairway. I continued to grin at her. I hoped I looked like Banquo's ghost. I hoped that every time she prepared to swing, she would see my smiling mug in her mind's eye.

Before she turned to go, she spat, very unladylike, in my direction.

TWENTY

Most of the gallery followed their heroine down the first fairway. I noted a few dirty looks from some of Big Wyn's staunchest fans. Obviously, any enemy of Big Wyn was an enemy of theirs, too. I just smiled at everyone.

Once the crowd thinned out, only about a dozen people were left outside the ropes. Looking across the tee box, I saw Harold Stilwell standing in the meager shade of a palm tree, wiping his brow with a handkerchief.. He was wearing his denim coveralls and a white T-shirt, looking every inch the country mechanic he had once been. He was staring thoughtfully down the fairway at the crowds chasing after the fast-striding form of his wife.

I sauntered around to his tree. He looked up.

"Buy you a beer?" I asked.

"You do and I'll be your friend for life," was his reply, and we headed for the nearest concession stand.

I glanced at the electronic scoreboard as we skirted the eighteenth green. Patty Sheehan and Beth Daniel were tied for the lead at four under par, but both were still on the back nine. Betsy King wasn't far behind and Maggie Wills, a coltish young blond from Florida, was also hanging around the lead.

I paid five dollars for two luke-cold plastic cups of beer and we found a nearby table with an umbrella that afforded a little bit of shade but not much relief from the humid afternoon sun. We sipped our beers in silence for a while, watching other people doing the same. From time to time, echoes of cheers and applause drifted in from various corners of the golf course. I felt that peculiarly charged atmosphere that accompanies a professional golf tournament. It's created, I think, by the unnatural silence that the fans adopt before a player makes a shot. There must be something about that collective inholding of breath that makes the air crystalline and brilliant, and the subsequent bursts of cheers and applause sound so loud and ringing. It's an atmospheric condition that seems unique to golf.

I looked over at Harold. "You follow Big Wyn out on the course much?" I asked.

He started, sitting a bit more upright, as if my words startled him out of some kind of reverie.

"Wha—? Oh, well, sometimes yes, sometimes no," he said. "I don't usually bother going out to watch the first round anymore. If she's in the thing on Sunday, I'll be there."

"Does she know if you're in the gallery or not?"

He grunted, once. "Wynnona Stilwell knows everything about everything that's going on around her," he said with a small, sad smile. "She's concentrating on her golf for sure, but I've seen her come off the course and tell the maintenance people to go rehang the gallery ropes that are down on the left of the sixth hole, and to move the portajohnnies on sixteen back a bit, and about a little puddle on twelve that should be marked 'ground under repair.'" He took a long sip of beer, leaving a foamy mustache on his upper lip. "I don't know how she does it, but she does. So to answer your question, yes, she does know when I'm there."

He looked out at the passing crowd. "She seemed to be in a peculiar mood today," he said thoughtfully. "I dunno, kind of preoccupied. I don't expect that she'll play very well. I've never seen her like this."

"Maybe it's Benton's death that's got her down," I suggested.

"Could be, could be," Harold nodded. "Too bad about ole Bergy. Kind of a dandy, and he drank too damn much, but I liked the man. Too bad."

"Did you know him well?" I wondered.

"Nah, not really," Harold shook his head. "Bergy didn't come to a whole lot of tournaments himself. Mostly just the majors and a handful of others. And when he did show up, he usually kept to the background. Especially after —"

Harold stopped abruptly, catching himself.

"After what?" I pressed. "What happened to him?"

He took another long swallow of beer. He put his cup carefully back on the table, slowly, then turned and looked at me. He shook his head back and forth, slowly. I got the message. He wasn't talking.

"Did he ever say anything to you about resigning? About being upset with…the way things were being run?" I knew better than to personalize the question. Harold Stilwell was a loyal husband and wouldn't take kindly to insinuations about his wife.

"Nah," he said. "Like I said, he didn't talk to me much over the years. Mostly hello, goodbye, nice to see ya. Well, once, it was quite a few years ago, he came to me and started to complain about something Wynnona had decided. I sat that boy down and told him I was a retired man and did not work for the LPGA in any capacity whatsoever and that if he had a problem with Wynnona, he should bring that problem up directly with Wynnona." Stilwell smiled at the memory. "He got the message, I do believe, because he never troubled me with anything but small talk again."

It was my turn to pause and sip a little beer. Stilwell knew what hold Big Wyn had on Benton, but he wasn't telling. And I wasn't sure how to get him to do so. I could try throwing him to the ground and twisting his ear until he cried 'uncle,' but I might get arrested for elderly abuse.

"Tell me, Hacker," he interrupted my train of thought, and not a moment too soon. "You ever wished you could be somebody else?" He leaned forward, elbows on the table. "You know, just kind of melt into the crowd, disappear, and come out as somebody new? Start over…new life…do something completely different? You ever feel that way?"

"Well—"I started to answer.

"'Cause I sure do, sometimes," he said.

This was new ground and I wanted to step carefully. There might be mines buried here. Or treasure.

"I suppose," I said, "If I was living a life that wasn't what I really wanted. If I was forced to do things I didn't want to do. Or if my life was pretty strictly run by someone else. Then I might feel like running away, yes."

"Damn right," Harold said.

"But I've always tried to make sure no one else was pulling my strings," I told him. "It's hard to do, and even I can't make it work all the time. But as long as they tell me it's still a free country, I intend on taking them at their word, and try to live my own life. As long as I don't harm anyone else, I try to make my own decisions."

Harold was silent, watching the people walk by.

"And I'd like to think that if I found myself in a situation where I couldn't make my own decisions, live my own life, answer mostly only to myself, that I'd be able to do something about it, short of just disappearing. Which is just one way of running away, you ask me. There are lots of ways to skin a cat, as they say."

He mumbled something.

"What?"

"Mumbo jumbo," he said. "Bunch a damn mumbo jumbo."

We lapsed into silence again. We were sitting in an area between the last green and the clubhouse. A group of players, coming off the eighteenth and heading for the clubhouse, pushed their way through the mingling gallery. At the front was Julie Warren, visibly sweaty and trailed by her caddie. When she was about thirty feet away, she caught sight of Harold and me sitting there drinking our beer and she deviated her path and headed straight for us.

A little girl clutching a white visor and a pen stepped in front of Julie and held the items up, asking for an autograph. Julie growled something at the girl under her breath and shook her head sternly. The little girl turned away with a look of shocked surprise.

"Hal, I don't think you should be talking with this guy," she said to Harold, jerking her thumb at me. "I don't think Big Wyn would like it."

Harold leaned back and looked up at Julie, cocking his head to one side. "I happen to be enjoying a cold brew with my friend here," he said slowly. "If it's any business of yours, which it ain't."

"He's out to get us, you old fart!" Julie shouted at him. "I'm telling you, don't talk to him!"

Harold Stilwell leaped to his feet, spilling his chair over backwards, and put his red and angry face right next to Julie's. "And I'm telling you to mind your own goddam business," he growled, his voice low and dangerous.

They stared at each other, eyeball to eyeball, for several long moments.

"I'm telling Big Wyn," she said finally.

"I'm supposed to pee my pants?" Harold retorted. "Go on, get outta here."

Julie Warren turned on her heel and stomped away. She didn't look at me, which is too bad, because I had on my best innocent angel look.

"Lovely woman," I said when she'd gone.

"Class A bitch," Harold muttered, righting his chair and sinking back into it.

I couldn't disagree, so I bought him, and me, another beer.

Thirty minutes later I was heading back to the press room to see if anyone had managed to catch either Sheehan or Daniels for the lead. Halfway there, I ran into Sybil Montgomery. She was just heading for the tenth tee, caddie in tow, to begin her first round. She slowed when she saw me and allowed her caddie to walk on by. I caught up to her.

She rested her hand lightly on my shoulder, her eyes fastened on mine. Quietly, with a pleasant little smile playing about her lips, she leaned over to whisper something to me. I bent down to hear.

"Cindy D'Angelo," she said and winked.

"Dinner tonight?" I answered. She laughed, her eyes dancing.

"Sounds lovely," she said. "I'll have to let you know. Tah-tah,dahling, off to war."

She gave my shoulder a little squeeze and headed off to the tee, her afternoon of work ahead. I watched her go and felt a nice tingle on the place where her hand had rested. It was a nice feeling, that tingle. I wanted more.

Sighing, I headed back to the blessed relief of the air conditioned press room, grabbed a beer from the cooler and plopped down in an empty chair to scan the scores. Daniel was now one stroke ahead of Sheehan, with a half-dozen others within four shots. Big Wyn had just bogeyed the eighth, I saw, and was now three-over for the day. Good.

When Honie Carlton walked in, I motioned her over with a wave, then led her to a quiet, out-of-the-way corner. I didn't want to be overheard.

"Need some research, kid," I said. "Former player named Cindy D'Angelo. Rookie about ten years ago, I'm told, was then pretty young, as in teens. I'd like to know about her and, if possible, where she is today."

"Okay," Honie said. "D'Angelo. Got it."

"And Honie, you have to keep this very quiet," I said seriously. "I mean top secret. It could be dangerous for both of us if anyone close to Big Wyn finds out what I'm doing."

She fingered the bandage wrapped around her noggin. "You got it," she said, turned on her heel and left.

God, I love to delegate. Especially when they obey without question. I felt good enough, having set some wheels in motion, to go get another beer from the press cooler and make it last at least five minutes.

I placed a call to Don Collier at hotel security, who told me that Bergmeister's autopsy was scheduled for sometime later that afternoon. He said he expected some results around six. But, he said, the police had unofficially put Benton's death down to natural causes, yet unknown, and had pretty much closed the case.

"How about his family? I asked.

"He has one daughter, is all," Collier said. "She asked to have his effects packed up and sent out to her in California. Someone from the Tour helped me with that this morning. I'm still trying to recover from the experience."

"How's that?"

"Let me put it this way," Collier said. "Hubba hubba to the nth degree."

"Oh," I said, "That must have been Casey. Did she bat her long eyelashes at you?"

"No, dammit," he growled. "I had to make the inventory list as she packed everything into the box. She was as cold and efficient as a stiletto."

"Yeah," I said, trying not to laugh, "I've heard she can be a tough nut to crack."

"But I can see where some might give their all in the attempt, though," he said and rang off.

Barley Raney walked over and perched his large buttock on the edge of my desk. "So, Hacker," he said jovially. "How do you like covering the ladies? You gonna defect from the PGA Tour and make this a full-time gig?"

I laughed. "Hell, Barley," I said. "Way too much politics and backstabbing going on for my taste. In the men's game, all they do is play golf."

He nodded sadly. "Yeah, I know what you mean," he said. "Get on the wrong side of someone out here, you get awful tee times, guaranteed spike-marked greens and crappy rooms. But you know what I hate the most?"

He screwed up his face in a look of intense disgust.

I waited.

"They're all so goddam nice to each other in public," he said. "They're always coming out with crap like 'Oh, Suzy played so well today, I am so happy for her!' when you know what they'd really like to do is take a three-iron and wrap it all the way around little Suzy's coconut!"

He sighed. "I just wish one of 'em would say something like "If little Suzy had drained one more impossible putt from the other side of the green, I would have taken my putter and crammed it sideways up her ..."

I interrupted Barley's fantasy with my laughter. He joined in.

Honie Carlton came back in, a big grin creasing her face. We headed back to our quiet little corner for another sotto voce discussion.

"Computers are wonderful inventions," she said. "They know everything."

"Give."

"She played on Tour for just three years," Honie said. "Quit about six years ago. Never won much money, but enough to keep her playing card. Was just seventeen when she turned pro. Probably burned out. It happens with the young ones."

"Yeah, that fits," I said. "Where was she from?"

"Florida." Honie smiled broadly again.

"Damn! That's great," I said. "Whereabouts?"

"Naples, originally."

"That's what, two hours from here?"

"She's closer than that," Honie said.

"How do you know?"

"Well, I had the contact number from her playing days. Got hold of her parents. They told me she's living some-place else these days."

"Where?"

"Right here," Honie said, still grinning. "Miami."

"Awesome!" I said. "Got her address?"

"As a matter of fact, I do," Honie said. She held up a slip of paper.

"Let me guess," I said. "She's working as an assistant pro at some country club."

"Wrong," Honie giggled. "She's a stripper in a titty bar in Coconut Grove. Place called La Doll House.'" She gave me the paper which had the address. "She, er, 'dances' inter-pretively under the name of Tawny."

She was giggling harder now, probably due to the look of amazement that must have been written on my face.

"Well," I said, taking the address and tucking it away in my shirt pocket. "It's a dirty job, but somebody has to do it."

"I thought you'd say that," Honie giggled.

TWENTY-ONE

Coconut Grove is one of Miami's nightlife gathering places. The nightclub district is filled with watering holes, elegant restaurants, desserteries, comedy clubs and other establishments that strive to attract some of the city's beautiful people away from the Parade o'Glamor that takes place over at Miami Beach's Art Deco district. One sees a lot of Don Johnsons and Melanie Griffiths on the make.

On the outer fringes of the Grove, however, the scene drifts decidedly downscale, and over by Miami University, where the subway runs overhead on its concrete stilts, one finds the workingmen's bars, fast-food joints and little bodegas, with their neon beer signs in the windows, music in the jukebox, and paisanos hanging around outside.

La Doll House was located in this part of the Grove. A huge garish sign dominated the streetscape while it tried to lure in the horny motorists from I-95. The sign featured a mostly naked woman, her hip cocked provocatively, arms thrown out invitingly, long blond hair positioned strategically. THE GROVE'S HOTTEST SHOW, it promised. Sounded good to me. I pulled my rental car into the crowded parking lot and joined a short queue waiting to get inside.

The cover charge was ten bucks, collected by a smiling hostess in a shimmery green dress that featured décolletage down to her navel. There was a neckless hulking bouncer standing nearby, his eyes completely hidden by thick, wraparound sunglasses. I resisted the impulse to go up and wave in front of his face, like the tourists do to the guards at Buckingham Palace. I was reasonable sure I didn't want to get a reaction from this guy.

"Two drink minimum, fellas," the hostess beamed at us, and she ushered us into her den of iniquity. The inside of the place was all mirrored walls and chrome-edged furniture, with deafening music and flashing strobe lights. A large central stage, made out of backlighted white Plexiglas, had twin runways branching out into a V-shape, with a chrome post extending upwards to the ceiling at the end of each runway. There were tables and chairs alongside each of the runways, and they were packed with the "gentlemen" who came to such places. Flanking the main stage, against the wall on each side of the large room, were chrome birdcage areas. There was a naked woman cavorting in each of the birdcages. Away in the back of the room, a silvery curtain led to what looked like a private viewing area. No doubt, the place for "private" dances, where extra cash bought extra services.

The noise was almost painful. The house DJ had the volume cranked up into the red zone. Scantily clad waitresses, dressed in push-up bras and fishnet stockings, bustled around taking and delivering drink orders. Bottle beer seemed to be the beverage of choice, so I ordered one. My waitress brought me two, and she leaned provocatively over to yell into my ear.

"That'll be ten bucks," she screamed. "Two drink minimum." I thought about telling her it was against my religion to pay more than three dollars for a bottle of beer, but figured she was probably too busy to sympathize.

I glanced around La Doll House, spending, of course, the requisite amount of time checking out the babes who were gyrating on the main stage and wrapping themselves provocatively around the chrome poles. With my finely tuned reporter's sense, I quickly noted that the ladies were quite naked and not unfortunate looking. The one on the stage nearest to me bent over and segued into a full split. It made me wonder if the stage were ever disinfected.

When I was finally able to tear my eyes away from the stage action and check out the rest of the place, I could see it was a good night: the place was busy. As in most strip joints I had ever visited – strictly for scientific if not journalistic reasons, of course – the all-male audience could be stratified into three basic categories.

First was the party crowd. Groups of men in full boys-night-out mode who were celebrating an upcoming wedding or someone's 50th birthday with much giddiness and aplomb. They were the ones who, within the safety of their group, felt secure (or were drunk) enough to do the whistling and yelling and motioning for the dancers to come over a receive a folded dollar bill in their garters. Or to be captured between the breasts. It was loud, noisy, sweaty and generally idiotic fun. The dancers put up with the party boys with wary good humor. These guys, after all, were throwing dollars around like, well, drunken frat boys, and were slugging down five dollar beers apparently unconcerned with the sacrilege involved. For the dancers, after all, it was a living, and these guys were the cash cows.

The second group was the regulars. These were guys who probably considered La Doll House their local pub, notwithstanding the high cost of beer. The local neighborhood tavern, albeit a little noisier, a little flashier and, oh yeah, with a bunch of young and naked females flaunting their sexual organs in public. The regulars sat and drank quietly with studied nonchalance and general disinterest. They had seen it all, many times before.

Finally, there were the strange ones. The quiet watchers. These men sat there with small, self-deprecating smiles as if they were enjoying this healthy male outlet but in their haunted eyes, even in the neon-colored gloom of the place, one could see pain mixed with desire and the entire range of stunted human sexual emotion. But only in their eyes, which were locked on the gyrating bodies in front of them. The watchers would sit there unmoving, their five-dollar beers turning warm and flat and untouched, while their creepy eyes drank in the buttocks and breasts that bounced and twirled and flashed in front of them. It was quite hypnotic, and after a set of dancers had finished their three-song sets and pranced off backstage, one could often see the watchers blink rapidly, sit up suddenly, breaking free from their mesmerization, glance around sheepishly, rub their eyes and then, as the next group of dancers appeared, sink back into the spell of flesh.

The waitresses hustled, the dancers stripped, the music attacked the ears. Two hostesses dressed in short sequined minis, walked through the place, trying to sell table dances. For an extra fee, usually twenty bucks, one of the dancers would perform a strip right at one's seat. It was kind of a private performance that everyone got to watch. Some of the party boys had bought one for their buddy. The girl came out, made a big fuss over meeting everyone, and sat in the man's lap, tickling him under the chin and whispering naughty things in his ear. Then, she got up and, with the music as her guide, began to dance and peel off her teddy and then her panties, keeping a light hand on the man's shoulder or knee, showing him everything and letting him touch nothing. One of the neckless bouncers was always nearby, implacable behind the shades, ready to pounce the instant a man's hand strayed someplace where it was not welcome.

I motioned one of the hostesses over to my table, where I sat alone.

"Hey fella, felling lonely?" she purred, smiling at me.

"Yeah, kinda," I said. "Is Tawny working tonight?"

"I think she comes on in a couple of hours," the girl said. "Anyone else you got in mind?"

"Nah, I'd really like to see Tawny," I said. I slipped her a twenty dollar bill.

She smiled at me with cold, seen-everything eyes. "Sure hon," she said. "Have a few drinks. Enjoy the show. I'll speak to her when she gets in."

It was more than two hours before Tawny got there. In the long, long interval, I did what everyone else in La Doll

House was doing: watching the girls. I saw all the body types as they came out in tandem to perform. There were the huge, probably surgically enhanced, big-breasted types; the skinny, barely anything on top types, and most every variation in between. Some of the girls ran a little toward the chubby side, but others had hard, lithe bodies that showed off a lot of hard work in the gym.

They were all smiling. It is their job to smile. Look, their smiles say, we're so happy to be naked, so all you pitiful men can get an eyeful. They adopted that Playboy bunny pursed lips thing, too, that pouty, mock-sexy thing that's supposed to convey passion.

But don't look at their eyes, because that's the ultimate buzz kill in a titty bar. The eyes always betray them. The eyes say they know they're contributing to human depravity and they don't like it one bit. The eyes say they hate it, actually. The eyes are dead and cold and hard. The eyes say a girl has to earn a living somehow, so go ahead and look you pigs, you filthy, low-life, disgusting animals.

The bodies may have been arousing, but the eyes deadened the thrill. I tried to navigate between arousal and disgust with the help of about six high-priced beers. I was thinking it was time to upgrade to Scotch when a soft hand tapped me on the shoulder and I turned to face Tawny, nee Cindy D'Angelo, professional golfer.

She was a striking woman, on the tall side, with straight blond hair that hung down to frame her face. It reminded me a bit of Maryann Faithful and the Sixties. The blond went dark at the roots. She was wearing a purple teddy with pearl snaps down the front, where her large breasts strained against the thin material, her nipples making two soft dents.

The teddy thing flared out below her waist in a very abbreviated skirting, beneath which I caught glimpses of a matching thong. Her figure was trim, but I could still see what had once been an athletic form in it. Her legs were still strong and muscular and betrayed the baby-doll look she was striving for. Her face, like the other girls', was heavily made-up and mascaraed, and she had applied some purple sparkling streaks around her cheekbones, giving her face a garish, yet exotic appeal. Her eyes, of course, were dead and cold.

"I understand you've been waiting for me for quite some time," she breathed at me, and bending down, grabbed my earlobe between her teeth and gave me a gentle little nip, finished by a sexy and soft moan. "You got any special requests?"

"I sure do," I breathed back, trying to look overcome with desire. "I want to spend a few minutes chatting with Cindy D'Angelo, former girl golfer."

She straightened up, eyes narrowing sharply, her lips turned into a disapproving frown. She gave me the once-over.

"You don't look like a cop," she said, all sexuality instantly gone from her voice.

"Nope, I said. "Worse. Reporter."

She blew out a breath that sounded like "pfaw," put a hand on her hip and stared at me angrily. "I don't do interviews," she snapped.

"It's not an interview," I said. "I just need some background information." She looked dubious. "Really," I tried not to sound pleading. "I just need five minutes. Your name will never hit print. Please?"

My mother was right. Manners are important. Tawny blew out another breath and motioned at me to follow her. She led me to the back of the bar, through the gauzy curtains into the private area. Inside, there were about six tiny grottoes, filled with pillows and soft chairs, where one could go with a girl, pull the screen, and, for the right price in cold hard cash, satisfy your every desire. As long as it didn't include touching or actual human contact. There was yet another neckless bouncer standing against the back wall of the private area, his arms folded, his face impassive, his eyes covered by his shades.

Tawny led me to the last compartment. She stopped at the entrance to the little room and held out her hand.

"Forty bucks," she said. "That'll get you five minutes."

I placed two twenties in her hand, she shoved me inside and followed, pulling the fabric screen closed behind her. "Okay," she growled. "Whaddya want?"

"How'd you get the neat name?" I asked.

She rolled her eyes. "My manager," she said. "And I suppose you want to know how a nice girl went from the wholesome fairways of the professional golf tour to being a stripper. Well, I make a whole lot more money doing this with a whole lot less effort. So to answer your question..."

"I didn't ask," I said quietly.

She stared at me for a moment, her anger barely under control. Then she smiled. It was a pretty smile, even underneath the strange purple sparkly stuff, and even with the still-hard cold eyes.

"Sorry," she said. "I guess I was jumping to conclusions. What's your name, anyway?"

"Hacker," I said and held out my hand for her to shake. "Boston Journal."

"So where'd you get the neat name?"

We laughed together, the ice finally broken.

"So," I said. "How did a nice girl go from the wholesome fairways …"

She laughed again. "Say," she said. "Do you think you can get a couple of passes for Sunday? I haven't seen the girls play in person now for a few years."

"Consider it done," I said. "You want them left under the name of Cindy or Tawny?"

"Cindy's fine," she smiled. "So what can I do for you, Mr. Hacker?"

"I don't know if you heard, but Benton Bergmeister died last night." I watched her face for reaction. Did her eyes widen a fraction at the name? I couldn't tell for sure in the dimly lit surroundings of our pleasure palace. I guessed that years of practice in disguising her emotions at a place like La Doll House might have helped.

"Oh, that's too bad," she said noncommittally. "He was a nice old guy."

"Yeah, I thought so too," I said. "Anyway, I'm here because there is a rumor that Benton had some deep, dark secret in his past, and the rumor says that you are it."

"I see," she said. Her eyes had turned to ice.

"I thought I'd track you down and let you comment on those rumors, if you want," I said. "You don't have to say anything. I'll go away and leave you alone. Or you can help me out and tell me what happened between you two."

"And what's in it for me, Hacker?" she snapped angrily.

I shrugged. "Nothing that I can think of," I said. "Maybe a little peace of mind, putting to rest something that may still be troubling you?" It sounded lame even to me.

Tawny chewed on her lower lip and stared off into space. Finally, she turned and looked at me.

"Hell, if the guy's dead, I guess it doesn't matter any more, does it?" She sank down into one of the chairs, closed her eyes and began to talk.

"I turned pro when I was seventeen," she began. "I know now that was way too soon, but I thought at the time I had the world by the short hairs. I was all-everything here in Florida. I don't think I could have shot anything above 75 if I wanted to. It was all that easy. I beat all the girls my own age, and then I beat all the college girls. I even trimmed Kathy Whitworth in this exhibition match when I was sixteen. Only found out later she had the flu that day. I was the youngest semifinalist in the U.S. Amateur...ever! Everybody said I was 'can't miss' and I believed them."

She opened her eyes and smiled at me, rueful. "So I decided to turn pro. Why go to college? I could already beat those girls. I decided making lots of money was a much better idea than going to classes for the next four years. Besides, I was 'can't miss!' Cindy D'Angelo, the Florida Schoolgirl! The next great thing.

"But it was too soon. I was naïve. Innocent. Hadn't finished growing yet. My body changed and my swing changed with it, and I lost it completely. Couldn't drive it in the fairway, couldn't get my irons onto the green, couldn't putt a lick. I had been given five tournament exemptions – I was good PR for the Tour after all – and I missed the cut on the first three.

"That's when Benton stepped in a tried to help. He saw what was happening and took me under his wing. Kept me away from the press, assigned another girl to room with me and show me the ropes, and tried to spend some time with me whenever he could, trying to keep me relaxed and focused on playing good golf again."

She opened her eyes and looked at me. Her eyes were wet and shiny.

"He was really being nice to me," she continued. "And it started to work. I calmed down, made some cuts, got invited to more tournaments. I started to play better, and felt my confidence coming back. Then, one night, he jumped me."

"Jumped you?" I echoed stupidly.

"We went out to dinner. He'd been drinking before, and kept drinking during and after. He was walking me back to my room when he suddenly turned and pounced. Drunken kisses, hands everywhere, ripping my clothes. It was pretty awful."

"How'd you escape?" I asked. "Swift kick to the cojones?"

She laughed. "Naw, I told you. I was just an innocent schoolgirl. I never even saw it coming. It was just luck that coming down the sidewalk that night was Wynnona Stilwell. She saw what was happening and came over to stop him."

"Big Wyn," I sighed.

"Yeah," Tawny nodded. "Lucky for me, I guess. Unlucky for Benton. She was breathing fire at him when she pulled him off. He immediately went all contrite and started to cry. He was just drunk on his ass. God, what a scene." She shuddered.

"What happened next?" I asked.

"Well, the next day, Big Wyn came to see me, with a lawyer. She had some papers for me to sign. Said they were my agreement not to sue the Tour for sex abuse and that if I signed, she'd take care of me."

"Take care, meaning?"

"Extra perks and bennies," Tawny said. "Good rooms, good tee times, upgrades to first class on flights, stuff like that. In return, I was not to think about suing either the Tour or Benton Bergmeister. Hell, I never even thought about doing something like that anyway. He was a nice old guy, just a drunk who got lecherous. All I wanted to do was forget the whole thing and go play golf. So I signed both papers."

"Both?"

Tawny smiled at me with approval. "You're quick, Hacker. I'll give you that. Yeah…two papers. I remember glancing at the first one and reading some of the legal stuff in there. It said about what Big Wyn had told me. So I signed it and the paper under it, just like the lawyer guy said to. It was a couple years later before I learned that second document wasn't anything like the first one."

"What was it?" I asked.

"Basically, it was an affidavit that I had been attacked and was planning to press charges against Benton Bergmeister for assault and battery, attempted rape and transporting a minor across state lines for immoral purposes. And a few other things too." She smiled at me grimly.

"But you said you didn't want to press charges, but forget the whole thing!"

"Exactly," Tawny said. "Big Wyn and her snarky lawyer managed to get my signature without my knowing what was going on. Once they had that document, which they later got notarized to boot, they had Benton Bergmeister by the balls. They apparently showed it to Benton and told him that I wanted to prosecute him for rape, but that Big Wyn had convinced me to hold off for the good of the Tour. And that as long as Benton did what Big Wyn wanted, she would continue to protect his sorry ass from the press and the publicity, not to mention the jail. But if he didn't …"

"I'd have called her bluff," I said. "They couldn't have made that stand up in court."

Tawny smiled at me. "You men are so macho," she said. "Benton did call her bluff. At least, that's what I heard later in the locker room gossip. He supposedly told her she couldn't do that to him."

"What happened?"

"Big Wyn sent the signed and notarized statement to Benton's wife."

"Jeezus."

"Who immediately filed for divorce, got a large settlement and refused to let Benton see his own daughter ever again." Tawny stared at me coolly. "Benton wasn't so macho after that," she said. "In fact, it was right about then that he started getting drunk at about noon every day."

I thought about Big Wyn's strange and triumphant look when Bergmeister's family had been mentioned in the press room. Now I knew why she had looked so victorious. She had beaten this man, destroyed his life, disrupted his family. Pretty good day's work.

"And you never knew about this?" I wondered.

She shook her head. "Naw," she said. "I went back to playing golf, but I never quite got over the hump. Benton couldn't spend time with me any more, for obvious reasons. So I slid back into mediocrity. Oh, I had some fun, made some friends, struggled like mad, never made much money, and after three years, I just walked away. " She stared off in the distance.

"I think I really missed what Benton had given me," she said. "Confidence, peace of mind, I don't know, maybe just friendship. But I burned out on everything. Knocked around for a couple years doing this and that. Waitress. Boat rat. Didn't even pick up a golf club. My parents eventually threw me out. I ended up working at places like this."

She turned to look at me, her eyes now large and sad. "It's pretty good money," she said, daring me to deny it. "But I miss golf. And the Tour. I had some really good friends. But I lost touch with them all." She sighed.

"Did you ever get all those perks Big Wyn promised?"

"Yeah, she took pretty good care of me," Tawny said. "No complaints."

"She ever come on to you?"

Tawny looked at me with a strange smile. "Hacker, you've got a dirty mind," she laughed, mirthlessly. "Or you've been talking out of school to someone. To answer your question, no, not really. She let it be known that she was available for sex if I wanted. But I was just a kid and really hadn't gotten into sex at all. I mean, I knew about lesbians and about Big Wyn and the others. You learn pretty quick out there. But I was just into golf and not much else."

I looked at the girl for a moment, turning something over in my mind.

"Listen, Cindy," I said. "I know I said I just needed some background. But it would help if you agreed to go public with this."

She was shaking her head.

"No way, man," she said. "I don't want to become a public figure, tabloid queen or go on Jerry Springer. It might be hard for someone like you to understand this, but this is a pretty good job. I like my friends here, we all look out for each other. There's no heavy lifting, the hours are good and the money can be damn good if you know what you're doing. I'm not about to rock the boat by becoming your star witness. No thanks."

"Look," I said. "Benton's dead. I still don't know exactly how or why, but he don't care. I believe Big Wyn is behind it, somehow. That woman has ruined a bunch of lives, including, indirectly, probably yours. I think it's time someone said stop. I can start the ball rolling, but I gotta have a source or two. You're it. You're the hold she had on Benton, which drove him to death. Think about it. He apparently gave up. I'm not going to. I need your help."

She was chewing on her bottom lip nervously as I gave her my best freedom-of-the-press sermon. Hold high the banner of truth and all that.

It might have been working, but just at that moment a huge, sunburned man in a sleeveless T-shirt and dirty jeans staggered into our private cubicle. His face was shaggy with several days' beard, his eyes were unfocused, he smelled of hard liquor. He had a large gut, flabby arms and brown leather cowboy boots.

"Omigod," he gasped, staring at Tawny in her purple teddy. "Honeybunch, you and me got some serious dancin' to do. C'mere!"

He lurched forward and his big beefy hands grabbed the front of her teddy and pulled it apart. It happened so fast, she didn't have time to react until he was pawing her breasts and making strange mewing sounds.

"Hey!" I yelled and started beating on the guy's back, trying to grab his arms and pull them away. Tawny let out a bellow of rage, and out of the corner of my eye, I saw a blur of black as the bouncer, moving far quicker than a man of his size should be able to, moved in. With one hand, he shoved me down into a chair, with the other he smashed a forearm into the drunken fool's beefy neck. The drunks' head and shoulders came up in surprise at the sudden pain. That gave Tawny the opportunity to get a knee free, which she brought up sharply into the man's groin. At the same time, the bouncer slipped his arm under the guy's chin and began applying pressure, choking off his oxygen.

A second black-clad bouncer burst into the room, picked me up out of the chair, off my feet, whirled me around and smashed me face first against the wall. He grabbed my arm and twisted it painfully up behind my back. "Go ahead, motherfucker," he said softly into my ear. "Resist me. I haven't broken an arm in almost a month and I'm starting to get restless."

"Lay off him Rocky," Tawny called out. "It wasn't him. We was just talking when this boozer staggered in and started pawing at me."

The drunk had passed out and lay face first on the floor. He started to snore. Rocky reluctantly let go of my arm, and

I turned around, checking to make sure all my teeth were still intact. Tawny was examining her breasts and wincing.

"Goddamn it," she said as she fingered each one of her breasts unself-consciously. "Son of a bitch grabbed so hard he left bruises. Shit!"

"Baby, are you okay?" wailed a soft, feminine voice from just outside the cubicle. One of the other dancers ran in and gave Tawny a big hug. She had lots of curly red hair piled atop her head and wore a white stretchy number and high heels. "What happened, baby, are you OK? Do you need to see a doctor?" The redhead hugged Tawny close and then turned to look at the two bouncers standing there.
"Where the hell were you guys?" she snapped. "You're supposed to protect us, goddam it. She coulda been hurt!"

"It's okay, Doris, calm down," Tawny said. "I'm fine. Just a run-in with a drunk with fast hands. I may be wearing his fingerprints on my tits for a couple days. That's all."

"Oh, baby, how awful!" Doris wailed. "You come back with me right now and let me look. I've got some lotion that should help. And some pancake that should hide the marks. C'mon baby, I'll make you better. You know I can."

Doris slipped her arm around Tawny and began to lead her away.

"Cindy?"

I threw my hands out in appeal.

She looked back at me once. "Okay, Hacker," she said. "For Benton's sake."

"I'll leave you some tickets," I said. "Thanks."

She nodded and turned to go with Doris. I saw her rest her head gently on the other woman's shoulder and slip her own arm lovingly around the waist of Doris.

The two bouncers watched the women go. "Shit," one of them growled. The other bent over, grabbed the snoring, bloodied drunk by the belt and the scruff of the neck and effortlessly hauled him out the door. The other one glared wordlessly at me, so I left, under my own power.

TWENTY-TWO

When I got back to the hotel at around half past nine, the message light on my phone was blinking. I called the operator who told me that Don Collier had called. I dialed the extension for the security office.

"Ah, Hacker," he said, "Where you been?"

"Sampling some of Miami's most elegant nightlife," I told him.

"Well, there have been all sorts of interesting developments," he informed me.

The autopsy on Benton Bergmeister had taken place that afternoon. The medical examiner had found that Benton's blood alcohol level was right through the roof. He had apparently downed most of that bottle of Scotch the evening he died. No surprise there. But that hadn't killed the man…at least not by itself. It was the Nembutal interacting with all that booze that had killed him.

"Nembutal?" I said. "Isn't that like a sleeping pill or something?"

"Yeah," Collier said. "A depressant. Used as a sedative. Not good to mix with alcohol. It'll kill ya."

I thought for a minute. "Bergmeister must have known that," I said. "He wasn't stupid. So that means he either killed himself or, drunk, he accidentally swallowed the wrong pills."

"Well, it's not quite as simple as that," Collier told me. "I went back and checked my inventory…you remember the list I made when I was trying not to stare down that woman's dress?"

"And?"

"And none of the medications she packed up was Nembutal. He was taking stuff for his ulcer, high blood pressure and cholesterol, but he didn't have any sedatives in his room."

"Nothing he was taking would interact with a snootfull of booze?"

"Not according to a doc I talked to at the morgue," Collier said. "But the lab will do a complete analysis as soon as they get the pills back."

"Back?"

"Yeah, that bombshell from the Tour had already mailed them off to the guy's daughter in California, along with the rest of his stuff from the room. It will take a few days for them to get out there and then get sent back."

"Damn," I said. Unanswered questions. Then I thought of something.

"A couple days ago, Benton mentioned to me that he needed to have a prescription filled," I said. "If he did, there's got to be a record of it somewhere that we can check. Find out what he got and when it was filled."

"Shit, Hacker," Collier groaned. "There's gotta be a thousand pharmacies within a mile of this hotel. You want me to tell the cops to start calling each one?"

"Isn't there one that the hotel recommends when a guest asks?" I wondered. "I'll bet that he went there."

"Hmmm. Not bad, Hacker. I'll check into it." Collier rang off.

I sat in my room for a while, thinking, turning ideas over in my head. I picked up the phone and called the Dade County Medical Examiner's office, and after waiting for half and hour to get through to the right person, confirmed the basic information that Collier had given me. Death had been due to the hyper-depressive action of Nembutal combined with excess amounts of alcohol in Benton's system. His organs had basically been depressed into silence. Pending further investigation, Bergmeister's case was still open.

I pulled out my laptop and began to write. Sometimes, when I need to step back and take a clear look at a problem, I go ahead and compose a first draft. Then, re-reading, I can see where the biggest holes are in my story and can figure out how to plug them. After a half-hour, this is what I had:

> *Benton T. Bergmeister, the commissioner of the Ladies Professional Golf Tour who died suddenly yesterday in Miami, had been blackmailed for more than ten years by one of the Tour's most famous players, the Boston Journal has learned.*

In a stunning revelation, sources indicated that allegations of sexual misconduct by Bergmeister had long been used against him to ensure his continued allegiance and support for the policies of Wynnona Stilwell, the president of the LPGA Player's Council and one of the most accomplished players in the history of golf.

The story was confirmed by Cindy D'Angelo, a former golfer on the LPGA Tour who was the victim of the decade-old alleged sexual attack by Bergmeister. Ms. D'Angelo, who is now a dancer in a Miami nightclub, said she was duped by LPGA officials, including Ms. Stilwell, into signing a document which was allegedly used to blackmail the commissioner and ensure his cooperation.

Bergmeister, 64, died suddenly Thursday in his hotel room in Miami, where the LPGA is staging its Miami Classic golf tournament this weekend.

The circumstances surrounding his death have yet to be officially confirmed, but the Journal has learned that an unusual change in Bergmeister's medication may have been responsible for his death.

According to an autopsy performed by the Dade County Medical Examiner yesterday, Bergmeister's death was attributed to a fatal combination of alcohol and the drug Nembutal, a barbiturate.

While Bergmeister was known as a heavy drinker, investigators in Miami are trying to trace the source of the Nembutal, a medication not among those prescribed for Bergmeister. Police do not know how Bergmesiter got the drug or why he took it.

Sources within the LPGA have painted a picture of that organization as being under the firm control of Mrs. Stilwell, who has been a member of the Tour since 1965 and president of the policy-making players' council for the last thirteen years.

Re-reading it, I knew I had more than a few holes to fill and assumptions that needed confirmation. I also knew I'd eventually have to get Big Wyn's reaction. I glanced at my watch and decided it was too late to call her for a quote. And since all hell would undoubtedly break loose once I did, I wasn't all that unhappy about letting it wait until tomorrow. I read the piece to myself one more time, this time trying to imagine what Frankie Donatello, my editor up in Boston, would think as he read it. He'd once been a helluva reporter himself, but once they move upstairs and plop their ever-widening butts into one of those cushy executive chairs, they seem to lose about nine-tenth of their guts. Every other word out of their mouths suddenly becomes "liability" and "verifiable."

I was still working a few minutes later when I was startled by a rap at the door. I looked at my watch: just shy of midnight. When I opened the door, a waiter in a starched white coat stood in the hall, a heavily laden trolley in front of him.

"Room service," he said, smiling.

"You must have the wrong room," I told him. "I didn't order anything from room service."

"No, but I think you asked a girl out to dinner," said a soft female voice, and Sybil Montgomery stepped into view. I slapped my forehead. "Omigod, I forgot," I said sheepishly.

"Well, I didn't," she said smartly and pushed me aside. "Come along. Let the man work. I am utterly famished."

Sybil plopped down in a chair while the smiling waiter laid out the meal. She had ordered two steaks, salad, baked potatoes and a nice bottle of red merlot. It smelled heavenly when the waiter popped the metal covers off the plates. It occurred to me that I had eaten nothing all day except for all the beer I had downed at La Doll House. I was hungry, too.

"You are amazing," I told Sybil.

"Not at all," she smiled back. "I just know how to take care of myself. No sense waiting around for other people to do what I can very well do for myself."

"How'd you play today?"

"Not awful," she said, waving a hand dismissively. "Two under. I should think two more rounds the same would do very nicely."

"I should think rather," I tweaked.

The waiter finished and made to leave. "No ticket?" I asked. He said the lady had taken care of it. The lady smiled enigmatically at me. I slipped the guy a couple of dollars and he bowed out of the room.

As I opened the wine, I looked at Sybil and the dinner spread.

"You do seem to know how to take care of yourself," I said.

"Quite," she said.

"And you appear to get what you want," I mused. "Up to and including, it seems, me."

"What I want right now is dinner," she said. "First things first." She picked up her knife and fork and sawed into her steak.

"And after?"

Her chin jutted out. "Very bloody likely the same thing as you," she said defiantly, her eyes flashing angrily. "It is one of the primary human drives, you know. I do not apologize for that, nor do I feel it necessary to explain myself."

"No," I countered. "You don't have to explain. You just pop in and pop out when you feel like it."

She threw down her fork and stood up, her facing turning red. "Do you wish me to leave, Hacker?" she demanded, voice quavering with anger and embarrassment.

"No, Sybil," I said quietly. "I want you to stay. I just want more than your drives. I want to know the real you, the inside you. Not your bloody human drives."

Our eyes locked across the table. Slowly, she sat back down. Silently, I poured two glasses of wine. She took hers, sipped, replaced the glass and sighed.

"I'm sorry, Hacker," she said. "You are right. I was presumptuous. I am not used to opening up very much. This is such a nomadic experience most of the time, one learns not to dare. The people one tends to meet along the way are either horrible users or they're gone in a week's time."

"Like I will be," I pointed out.

"Yes, dammit, like you will be." She looked up at me, suddenly vulnerable, eyes shiny. "But I feel something different with you," she said. "Don't ask me why. Just a feeling. And that's a little scary for me to have, much less admit to."

I leaned over the table and clinked her wine glass with mine.

"Here's to scary feelings," I said. "And that wonderful, something-special feeling that goes with it. Because I have it too. So even though you'll be heading west on Monday and I'll go back to Boston, I think it's a good bet that our paths will be crossing again, soon. Because I don't get that feeling much, either."

She reached over and squeezed my hand. We didn't have to speak.

"What have you discovered about that Cindy person?" she asked me after a time.

I reached for my laptop, handed it to her, and showed her how to work the scroll keys. While she read, I attacked my steak. Whern she had finished, she sat back in her chair and looked at me thoughtfully, lips pursed.

"Will they run this?" she asked.

"I think so," I said.

"The feathers will fly," she said.

"I know."

"I'm not sure the Tour will survive," she said. "Sponsors may drop out. Everyone's sex life will become front-page reading. The networks will probably cancel our already pitiful schedule. Hacker, do you think this is wise?"

I looked at her. "Don't you think it's time somebody got Big Wyn's jackboot off your necks?" I asked. "Isn't it time for someone to step forward and say 'enough is enough?' Besides, what do you care if the LPGA falls apart? You can just trip on back to England."

"I don't think I deserved that," she said, her face showing hurt.

"I'm sorry," I said quickly. "That was low. Listen, I didn't ask to be the one to blow the whistle. But somebody is going to do it, sooner or later. And it's my job to report what I find. But somebody has to rescue this organization from that woman and make it work the way it's supposed to. I don't care if it's you or Mary Beth Burke or Nancy Lopez or Josephine the Cat. All I know is that Wynnona Stilwell's reign as the queen of terror is over."

She studied me. "I do hope you're right," she said.

TWENTY-THREE

I awoke early and lay in bed thinking while the rising sun filled the room with soft light. After a time, I leaned over and kissed awake the sleeping form beside me. Sybil stirred, moaned softly and finally opened her eyes.

"Sixty-nine," I said.

"Dear me," she said. "I don't know you quite that well yet, do I? Besides, didn't we already try that last night? Yes, I seem to recall ..."

To prove her point, she reached down beneath the sheet and stroked me. She was right.

"No, you boob," I laughed. "I just had an intuitive flash that you're going to shoot a sixty-nine today. The number came into my head and stuck there."

"Ah, well, I do hope you're right," she said. "In that case, will you just phone in the score for me? I'd like another hour of sleep."

"C'mon," I said, throwing back the sheets. "Up and at 'em. We have worlds to conquer."

I ordered breakfast to be sent to the room. We washed off each other's sticky parts in the steaming shower and threw on the hotel's soft terry robes. Breakfast came and we took it and the morning newspaper out onto the tiny balcony.

"I believe I'll need all of that sixty-nine today," Sybil murmured as she read through the results from yesterday in the sports section. "Beth Daniel did a sixty-six yesterday and she's been playing very well of late. Ah, well, off we go, then."

She gathered her things and, before leaving, came back out on the balcony for a farewell kiss. "Do be careful, Hacker dear," she whispered against my cheek. "The Queen is not yet dead and I fear she may have a few poisoned apples up her sleeve."

"Thanks for the warning," I laughed. "But I've got truth, justice and the American way on my side."

She kissed me again, looked into my eyes and left.

When I made it to the pressroom an hour later, I sat down and penned a quick note. Sealing it into an envelope, I sought out Honie, who was busy entering first-round statistics into a computer.

"Hey, Hacker," she said cheerfully, sitting back from her drudge work with a sigh. "How'd the search go last night?"

"Illuminating and eye-opening," I said with a straight face. She laughed out loud.

"Do you know what Big Wyn's schedule is today?"

"I think she had an early time today," Honie said, reaching for the pairing sheets. "Yeah, they went off an hour ago, so she should be finished right after lunch. Whaddya need?"

"I want you to tell her I need an interview with her ASAP," I said. "Private and one-on-one. And give her this." I handed her the sealed envelope.

"What is it?" Honie asked.

"Incentive," I said mysteriously.

I had some time to kill, so I went out on the course to watch some golf. I caught up with Betsy King's threesome on the front nine. Watching her play a few shots, I could see why she had been leading the money list for several years. Smooth, steady, her swing was classically correct, but looked a bit mechanical to me. She was all business out there. She pulls her visor down low over her eyes and you can feel her concentration. All her movements are deliberate, calm and unemotional. It's like watching a golfing machine at work: bloodless, cold and terribly efficient. She made a birdie at eight to pull within one of the lead.

I wandered on through the gallery. Cutting back over to the back nine holes, I happened upon Patty Sheehan's group. Looking at the sign carried by a young volunteer, I saw that Patty wasn't having the best of weekends. She had fallen to one under, eight shots behind. But watching her demeanor, you couldn't tell. Sheehan plays a game diametrically opposed to Betsy King's. She wears her heart on her sleeve for all to see. King walks slowly and deliberately from shot to shot, her eyes straight ahead, saying nothing. Patty practically dances down a fairway. I watched her hit a pulled drive that flew straight but down the left side, ending up in the rough, and for the first forty steps after it, she pulled her visor off and slapped her thigh with it, as if in self-punishment. But then she grinned to herself, popped the visor back on, looked over at the fans along the ropes, waved to a friend, slapped her caddie on the back and strode whistling in search of her ball. I followed.

The ball was lying up in the grass, which was lucky, but the fairway bent around to the left and three tall palms blocked her view of the green. She stood behind her ball for a moment, studying the options. Her caddie whispered the yardage and she nodded and pulled a club. While she was waiting for one of her playing partners to go first, she glanced over at the gallery ropes and saw me standing there.

"Watch this Hacker," she said with a grin. "Piece of cake!"

She took a couple practice swings, then stepped up to the ball. She had taken a long iron – it looked like a three – which was a dangerous club to play in the thick rough. But she made a typical Sheehan pass at the ball – smooth, rhythmic—and caught the ball cleanly.

It shot off down the right center of the fairway, low and hot, and began to curve sharply left, bending perfectly around the trees and the corner. Straining, I saw the ball land about thirty yards short of the green and start running with its hook overspin. It punched through the collar of bermuda around the green and then I lost sight of it. But the gallery around the green began to murmur and then roar as the ball trickled down the green, closer and closer to the hole.

Patty couldn't see where the ball finished, either, but from the cheers echoing down the fairway we could both tell that her miracle shot had finished close to the hole. She looked over at me with a huge ear-to-ear grin creasing her well-tanned face and I gave her a thumbs up. She threw her hands up in the air and waggled her legs in an excellent imitation of an NFL wide receiver doing a touchdown dance. The fans around me laughed and cheered.

Back in the pressroom an hour or so later, I got word that Big Wyn would give me half an hour at four. The message was relayed to me by Karla, the Tour's PR honcho and Honie's boss. I had not seen Honie since she left the pressroom with my message. Karla sought me out after lunch. She wore a conservative gray business suit with a colorful print scarf on the shoulder and a diamond-encrusted pin in the shape of a flagstick.

"May I ask the purpose of your interview with Mrs. Stilwell?" she asked, somewhat coldly.

"You certainly may," I said gallantly, "But I won't tell you. It's between Wyn and me."

She didn't like that, of course, but I really didn't care. I put my face back into the newspaper I had been reading and propped my feet up on the desk.

That's probably why she gave me the cold shoulder treatment a couple of hours later when she came to escort me up to Big Wyn's suite. I was going to ask her if she liked being a high-paid escort, but she might have taken the question the wrong way. She was stonily silent, so I settled for whistling tunelessly as the private elevator whisked us upstairs.

When the door opened, I told Karla that I could find my way, and she stayed in the elevator as the doors closed with a whisper. I walked past the smoky mirrors, down the curving hall and out to the dramatic balcony overlooking the living room and the panoramic views of the golf course beyond. Down below, Big Wyn was sitting quietly by herself on the plush white leather sofa. She was looking at a scrap of paper that I recognized as the note I had sent earlier with Honie. I walked down the curving staircase and sat down in a chair next to the sofa.

She didn't look at me right away, so I had a moment to study her. Big Wyn looked tired. She had, of course, just finished her round for the day, but this was more than that. Her eyes were wrinkled at the corners and her face looked etched with fatigue. Her shoulders seemed to slope downwards sharply. This was not the confident, triumphant Wynnona Stilwell, conqueror of the fairways. This was a tired, aging and somewhat apprehensive old woman.

"So who's this Cindy D'Angelo?" she rasped at me finally. "Somebody I'm supposed to know?"

I looked at her. "That's good, Wyn," I said. "Denial. But it won't work. I've talked to the girl. I've got the story on how you blackmailed Benton. It's a good one, too."

"C'mon, Hacker," she laughed mirthlessly, shaking her head. "Who's gonna believe some cockamamie story from a nude dancer…a hooker, probably?" She looked at me. "It'll go down as the rambling of some cheap little bimbo trying to score some big bucks from the Tour. Who's gonna compare her to what I've …"

She broke off suddenly and looked down at her hands. Then she got up and shiffled over to the big, floor-to-ceiling windows which overlooked the golf courses and crowds of spectators milling around. She stared out at this tableau, which she had helped create, and the late afternoon sun turned her silver-streaked hair a subtle hue of gold.

"You don't get it, do you Hacker?" she said softly. "I have worked my entire life for the girls on this Tour. I've worked like hell to get the money up so we can make a living. I've traveled the country back and forth twenty times finding places where we can play. I've worn out shoes tromping around New York, trying to get the networks to pay us some attention. I have kissed so much ass…"

She broke off, staring. I kept silent.

"You don't know the fights I had to go through," she continued. "In public, when the cameras are on and the reporters are there, they all say we're great athletes, fine people, the world's best female golfers. But in the back room, when the dollars are on the table, we're bitches and dykes and cunts…you name it, I've been called it. Every goddam name in the book, they've called me."

She ran a hand through her hair.

"Until I came along, these girls played for peanuts. For nuthin'! And they did it gladly, too, because they loved the game. When I came along, I said to hell with that! If we're gonna put on tournaments and entertain the folks, we're gonna get paid a fair dollar to do so. And it has been a fight, every step of the way. The PGA Tour…they throw money at those sons-a-bitches. But I had to fight for every dollar, for every perk, for every last thing we've got on this Tour."

"I do know, Wyn," I said. "I know it's been tough and I know you've done a hell of a job. But you've become part of the problem, not the solution. And you haven't always played fair."

"Fair!" She wheeled to face me, her eyes afire. "Fair? You think it's fair when the chairman of a major New York bank says he'll sponsor a tournament if I give him a blowjob? You think it's fair when one of my girls wins six tournaments in a row and Wheaties won't put her on the box? You think it's fair that our tournaments cost as much as the men's events, and we play for one-third the money? Fair? Don't talk to me about fair, Hacker. There's nothing that's fair in this life. Fair is what you make for yourself."

"Ah," I said. "The old 'ends justify the means' argument."

"You are goddam right," Big Wyn snarled, her face reddening. "I learned pretty damn quick that in this life you got two choices. You either get the other guy or he gets you. There's no in-between. I made up my mind early on that I was going to be doing the getting. Nobody was gonna get the better of Wynnona Haybrook in this life. Nobody."

I studied her for a moment. That defiant chin was jutting out, those fierce eyes sparkling. Big Wyn had put the chip squarely on her shoulder and was daring someone to knock it off.

There was a germ of truth in Wyn's impassioned claim. Women do have it tough, and women golfers trying to earn a living at their game were at a disadvantage. It wasn't fair, Big Wyn was right, but it was the way things were. Big Wyn certainly deserved credit for her efforts to try and make the playing field better, if not entirely level, for herself and the other players on the LPGA Tour.

But she had pushed the boundary. She had, in effect, made up the rules as she went along. She had kicked her ball out of the bunker, conceded herself long putts, not counted all the strokes. And not even the "not fair" excuse could justify that. She had not merely cheated, she had broken a trust. Whether for good or ill, the rules exist for a reason, and they cannot be ignored at will. At least, not without some consequence. In Big Wyn's case, there would be no one who would sign her scorecard.

"Wyn," I said. "I've gotta run this." I pulled out a copy of my story, unfolded it and handed it to her. "I understand what you're saying, but it's my job to run this piece. I'll include any comment you'd care to make."

Silently, she took the paper and read the story. She stopped only once, about halfway through, to look at me with her sad, weary eyes. When she had finished, she handed me back the paper and stared out the window into the afternoon.

"Comment?" I asked.

She mumbled something.

"Sorry," I said.

"Mumbo jumbo," she said. "Bunch a damn mumbo jumbo."

"That your comment?"

She waved her hand in dismissal. "Get back to you," she said. "Gotta think."

"Okay," I said. "But I'm sending this up to Boston in an hour. They'll want some reaction from you."

She waved me away again and I left her standing at the window, looking out at the wreckage of her life.

TWENTY-FOUR

I went back to the pressroom. The day's scores were being posted on the main scoreboard. Sybil had done one better, firing a nifty 68, putting her two shots out of the lead. I figured I'd call her for a congratulatory drink after I had filed the story.

I had missed her after-the-round interview session. Professional golf is probably the only sport in which the reporters covering the event can sit there and have the players brought in to them for interviews. Players who have shot particularly good rounds, and, of course, the leaders, come down from the locker room, sit on a raised dais holding a microphone and talk about their round. They usually start with a hole-by-hole, shot-by-shot description of birdies and bogies, and then we get to ask questions.

"So, how do you feel about tomorrow's round?"

"Well, I'm gonna try to stay in the moment, play one shot at a time."

Zzzzzz.

One of these days, before I retire, just for the hell of it, I'm gonna ask someone a doozy, such as "In Tolstoy's War and Peace, do you think Natasha represents the essential Russian mind?" Just to see what happens.

The room slowly emptied as the other reporters finished filing their stories. Barley Raney was reading a USA Today in one corner, while a half-dozen volunteer ladies in matching pink golf polo shirts bustled about, closing up shop for the day.

"Has anyone seen Honie Carlton?" I asked the ladies, who were setting out the final round's pairing sheets.

"Somebody said she's already left. Went up to Sarasota to get ready for next week," one of the volunteers told me.

I thought about that and frowned. She hadn't mentioned any plans to head of out town early. And she hadn't said good-bye, which was not like her at all. I was trying to decide if my feelings were hurt when the phone rang. The volunteer lady answered it and waved it at me.

"Hacker? Karla Donnelly, Tour PR," said the well-modulated voice. "Mrs. Stilwell has some responses to the allegations in your story and wants to give them to you."

"Fine," I said, getting out a sheet of paper. "Shoot."

"No," the voice said. "She wants to see you again in her suite. Right away."

"Aw, hell, can't you just read it to me?" I whined. "Save me the trip?"

"Ten minutes, Mister Hacker," and she rang off.

I groaned and swore silently to myself. If she was surrounded by her courtesans, the Queen would have regained her power and I would be in for some high-powered browbeating. Part of me, perversely, looked forward to the challenge. The other part of me wished suddenly for a direct flight to the Antarctic. I drained my beer, made an excellent, over-the-head hook shot into the wastebasket and headed for the door.

"Night, Hacker," Barley called out as I left. His head was still buried in the newspaper.

"Go home, Barley," I told him. "It's quittin' time."

"Yeah, right," he said.

The sun was fading fast in the western sky as I headed back towards the lobby. The last few streaks of orange and pink fought a losing battle against the deep blue tones that were fading quickly into black. I stopped for a moment and watched the darkening gloom as it swept over the golf courses. The gushing fountain in the lake beside the eighteenth green made a comforting sound, like the wind whistling through a mountain pass, as the rest of the world seemed to hush suddenly from the bustle and busyness of the day. The insects fell silent and the twinkling lights of the surrounding city began to blink on. The air was still and quiet and bathed by the night air. It had that soft quality that the zillions of tourists dream about when they think about Florida. It was soft and redolent and peaceful and most and sensual. It made me think about Sybil Montgomery. It made me feel alive, as night approached.

I breathed in that cool, delicious air and used it to refuel my resolve for what I was sure was going to be an acrimonious meeting with Big Wyn. I doubted I would be encountering the tired and worn-out Wyn in this meeting. It would, more likely, be the dragon lady.

Whoever got me was good, very good. I had not been paying much attention to things around me as I stood out on that terrace, enjoying the night air. But I never heard a thing. There was, suddenly, a burst of pain at the base of my skull, an explosion of bright and multi-colored light, and the sensation of falling and falling, end over end, into a deep black eternity.

It took me a while to convince myself that I had returned from that eternity, because when I came to I was still in a black and lightless void. It was the dull throbbing in my head that told me I was, indeed and unfortunately, alive. My hands were tightly bound behind my back and my shoulders began to chime in with the message that they, too, hurt like hell. I would have groaned aloud, but a gag had been pulled tightly across my mouth and tied behind my aching head.

It was dark, but I could sense I was lying in a smallish room. It was hot and airless. It was too dark to see anything identifiable. I seemed to be half-lying in a propped-up position on a hard daybed of some kind, my back wedged uncomfortably against a wall. The wall felt cool and smooth, and when I reached out with my bound hands as far as I could to touch it, it felt smoothly metallic in texture, like a kitchen countertop.

I strained in the dark to listen, trying to ignore the constant drumbeats of my throbbing head. I could hear nothing except a constant rhythmic buzz of insects. "Wherever I am, there's an outside nearby," I thought, and immediately credited myself with an amazing intuitive deduction. I tried struggling up into a sitting position and learned my legs had been hogtied at the ankles, too.

A wave of panic burst over me. Hands and feet tied, bound and gagged, dropped into an airless dark cell. "Okay, Commandant, I'll spill! Let me the hell out of here and I'll tell you anything you want to know! To hell with name, rank and serial number...just get me the hell out of here!" Hot tears of frustration and fear sprang up, and a rush of fear-based adrenaline caused me to sweat profusely, drops rolling down my back. The noise of my panicked gasps of air through my noise reverberated in the close little room.

Slowly, I got myself back under control. "Easy, Hacker," I cautioned myself. "You are not dead and if they wanted you dead, you would be alligator dinner by now. So relax, chill out, wait for the next act in this play. All you've got left is your brain, so use it."

I don't know how long intermission lasted. I may have dozed off. I may have sunk back into unconsciousness. I tried to let my mind wander to pleasant things. I thought about my beach cottage up on the North Shore, but that made me think of that scary next-door neighbor, and panic welled up in me again.

At some point, I finally heard a soft whisper close at hand. Then a door opened beside me, spilling harsh light into my small room. Almost at once, I realized why the wall behind me was smooth and metallic. I was in a motor home, the back bedroom compartment. In front of me was a bed, the twin of the one I was lying on, extending almost the entire width of the trailer. There was a small window to the right, tightly sealed with both blinds and curtains.

Harold Stilwell stuck his head in the door, looked down at me and grunted. "You're up, I see," he said. "Sorry about the ropes and such. Wynnona said she needs to talk to you and make you listen to some reason."

It was a good thing I was gagged. Had I been able to talk, I'm not sure what I would have said. But I suspected it would have been obscene.

Stilwell went away, leaving the door open. Cooler air flooded in, for which I was thankful. I didn't like the way I was beginning to smell. He was back in a minute.

"Listen," he said to me. "I don't really know why you gotta be all tied up like that, at least with the gag thingy. You could yell your fool head off out here and nobody's hear a thing, 'cept maybe a gator or two. Here, I brought you a beer. I'll take that thing out and help you drink it, and you promise to behave until Wynnona gets here. Deal?"

I nodded and he reached behind me and untied the gag. I spit the thing out and worked my jaws up and down, trying to relax the muscles.

"Here you go," he said and, holding the can of Budweiser out like he was feeding a baby, he poured some into my open mouth. I can't remember when anything tasted better."

"Thanks," I gasped.

"Don't mention it," he said and took a draught from the can he had brought for himself.

"Harold, what the fuck is going on?" I demanded.

He wiped his mouth with the back of his hand and shook his head.

"Now, Hacker, don't get started with me," he cautioned. "I told you...Wynnona needs to talk to you and she said this was the only way she could get you to listen. I don't like it much, tell you the truth, but Wyn said it's gotta be this way."

"Wyn is wrong, Harold," I said. "This is called kidnapping and assault. Both you and Wyn can go to jail. I would listen to anything Big Wyn had to say, but this is breaking the law."

He was silent, silhouetted in the light streaming in the door from the main body of the camper. He took another long pull of his beer.

"What has she got on you, Harold?" I asked. "She catch you sleeping with a young rookie, like Benton? She pay off your gambling debts? One thing I've learned this week, Big Wyn has something nasty on just about everybody around her. So what's she got on you, pal?"

"I don't know what you're talking about," he said sullenly.

"The hell you don't," I said heatedly. "She finds the weak link in everyone and pushes on it until it breaks. Once it does, she owns you. Forever. That's how she's run this organization for the last twenty years. That's how she controlled Benton Bergmeister until she killed him. That's –"

"Wynnona Stilwell did not kill Benton Bergmeister," Stilwell jumped up and yelled. "She's a fine Christian woman…"

"She's a witch, Harold," I said. "She likes to ruin other people's lives. I don't know what she has on you, but she runs your sorry life, too. Hell, she even got you to be an accessory to kidnapping! Don't tell me what a fine Christian woman she is."

Harold stood there, breathing heavily. He drained his beer and hurled the can away, where it clattered against the wall and floor. "I'm telling you, Hacker, you've got it wrong," he said, his voice cracking with emotion.

I decided to give him one more push.

"Okay," I said. "If you insist on being dickless…"

It was one shove too many. With a strangled cry of fury, Stilwell sprang at me, grabbed me by the throat and slammed my head backward, against the thin, metal wall. The light in the small room swam around and around and my consciousness went swirling with it, down and around and out the drain.

TWENTY-FIVE

A splash of cold water on my face pulled me up from the void. I opened my eyes and groaned at the assault of harsh light in my eyes. I had been moved into the larger compartment of Harold's motor home, the combination living room and dinette, where I had been plopped down on the built-in bench next to the small table. My head had been resting on the cold, hard Formica surface.

I groaned again and slowly rasied my head, wincing in pain. My hands were still bound tightly behind my back, my legs tied at the ankles. I leaned back against the backrest and looked around. Things were still foggy. The light from the overhead bulbs was unrelently harsh. I could hear a generator plugging away outside.

Harold Stilwell stood over me, holding an empty water glass. Standing by the entrance to the motor home was Big

Wyn, who stared at me with a combination of interest and hatred.

"Okay, Wyn, he's awake," Harold said. "I'm going outside and have a smoke." He fumbled in his overalls for pipe and tobacco and went out the door into the night.

Wynnona Stilwell took two steps toward me and stood there, towering above me. I raised my eyes upward at a painful angle to look back at her. There was an unmistakable aura of conqueror and vanquished in the little cabin of Harold Stilwell's motor home. Big Wyn's eyes were bright and clear and shone with power. I imagined those eyes looked the same on those countless afternoons when she had marched down the eighteenth fairway with another insurmountable lead, the cheers of her fans ringing in her ears.

"You have caused more trouble than you are worth," Big Wyn said to me now, her voice deep and sure and completely different from the wavering tones I had heard earlier in the afternoon. I looked closely at her again. Something had rejuvenated her.

"You have stuck your nose into places you shouldn't have," she continued. "You have made my life most unpleasant. Normally, I could deal with that. There have been other reporters who tried to do slam pieces on the Tour, even on me. I've taken my share of punches. It don't last. People forget about it. Life goes on. But you've gone too far, Hacker. You are a danger to everything I've worked for over the last twenty years. I can't let you do that."

"I haven't done anything, Wyn," I said. "You're the one who created this house of horrors. Now you have to live with the consequences. You're already in deep trouble. Don't make it any worse for yourself. Cut the crap, let me go and I'll tell the cops you came to your senses, no harm done."

She laughed. Threw back her head and laughed. It was a deep, throaty laugh mingled with madness. It sent a sudden chill down my back.

"Hacker, you don't know how much you sound like my father," she said now. "He was such a spineless little bastard who always tried to sound like a real man, a fighter. He tried to make us believe he was The Man, had all the answers, knew everything. He didn't know shit."

Her eyes had suddenly turned hot and bright.

"I was Daddy's little girl, or supposed to be. Be all cute and cuddly, wear pretty dresses, get married and settle down, raise a family. He had high hopes for me, his little girl. But I wasn't his little girl. I was always a tomboy. Always loved sports. Found out I was good at it. I could even beat the boys most of the time. Man, did that feel good!"

She was pacing now, back and forth in the contained space of the motor home.

"He never understood. He always said it was just a phase, that I'd settle down sooner or later and become a lady. Well, I knew I was never going to be a lady. I was going to be a champion. I was going to become the best golfer in the world. That was my dream. It was never his. One day, he came home from work early and saw me and my best friend kissing. Next day, he dropped dead of a heart attack."

She ran her fingers wearily through her graying hair. "He never understood. Never tried to."

There was nothing I could say. The sadness of Wyn's life swept over me, followed by despair. I was the prisoner of an unbalanced woman. I was in trouble.

"Anyway, Hacker, that's all in the past," she said, her voice regaining its edge. "Now it's all about you and the trouble you've caused."

"How many of your other press critics have you kidnapped and assaulted?" I asked.

She chuckled. "Never had to before," she said. "Most of 'em you can buy with a little bit of this or that and they go off their own way. But you weren't likely to do as you were told. I knew that from the day I laid eyes on you."

"Is that all this is?" I demanded. "A power struggle? Does that justify things like beating up Honie Carlton?"

Big Wyn shook her head with a frown. "Well now, I didn't really approve of that," she said. "I told Julie just to lean on the girl a little bit, make an impression on her. But Julie sometimes gets a little carried away. And I think she likes to hurt people. That can be useful sometimes."

I shook my head in wonder. "And what about Benton? He told me he was going to walk away from your little circus here. I'll bet he was going to blow a few whistles, too. Isn't it nice that he accidentally took the wrong pills on a full stomach of booze?"

She avoided my eyes. "Accidents happen," she mumbled.

"I don't suppose the lovely Casey Carlyle had anything to do with that accident?" I suggested.

She spun on me. "How did you know that?" she demanded. Then she halted, realizing what she had just admitted.

"Two plus two, Wyn," I said. "I know she's the general errand girl around here, as well as your main undercover agent. It makes sense that if Benton needed a refill on his prescription, he'd call Casey to have her go get it. The way I figure it, she went and got his scripts filled, and then got one for herself....probably a big bottle of Nembutal. I checked with the medical examiner. Both Nembutal and Minizide – which was what Benton was taking – come in nearly identical capsules. Hard to tell them apart, especially if you're drunk. I figure Casey switched the pills in the bottles and gave Benton the ones that eventually killed him."

"You can't prove that,' Hacker," she said.

"Maybe, maybe not," I shrugged. "The cops are checking all the drugstores around here, and they'll find out it was Casey who filled Benton's prescription. They'll find hers, too. I figure tomorrow they'll be hauling her lovely ass in for questioning. It won't look good, Wyn, not good at all."

The door to the motor home was suddenly swept open and Honie Carlton was pushed inside. She too had her hands tied behind her back and had a gag in her mouth. She looked at me with wide, frightened eyes and moaned once, softly. Coming in behind her, a vicious smile creasing her face, was Julie Warren, followed by Harold, who looked concerned.

Julie shoved Honie onto the bench opposite me. The girl was sick with fear and when she sat down, I could see the beginnings of fresh bruises on her face, and a trickle of blood at the corner of her mouth.

"Goddammit!" I yelled. "If you touch another hair on this girl's head, I'll have you thrown in jail for the rest of your sorry lives!"

Big Wyn laughed aloud and backhanded me with a solid swing of her meaty hand. My head rocked back against the wall and I gasped at the sudden, stinging pain. Moments later, I felt blood run out of my nose and begin to drip down onto my shirt. Honie shuddered and moaned again.

"You, my friend, ain't gonna do nothing of the sort," Big Wyn said to me menancingly.

"Here now," Harold Stilwell protested from the doorway. "There's no cause for that, Wynnona. You said you just wanted to talk some sense into this fella. You didn't say anything about …"

Big Wyn spun around and spat her words out. "Shut the hell up, Harold! Shut up! When I want to hear some goddam thing from you, I will ask. Until then, shut up!" She stared at her husband. He looked away.

"Wyn," I gasped, "This has gone far enough. You can't believe you'll get away with this. The story will come out. Barley Raney …"

"Barley Raney will do what he's told," Wyn snapped. "We know you haven't transmitted your story full of lies to Boston. We also know you work alone. So we'll take our chances that once you're out of the picture, the story dies."

"That's the plan?" I rasped. "You're going to murder Honie and me? Is it worth that much to you?"

Big Wyn just smiled her nasty little smile. She wheeled around, opened the door to a locker and reached inside. Turning, she held a shotgun, what looked like a Remington .365, over/under. Honie uttered another terrified moan when she saw the gun. I wanted to moan as well, but stifled it. Moaning is not manly.

"The story will be that horny ole Hacker here ran off with one of young assistant publicity officers," Big Wyn said. "You see, they were old friends, but Miss Carlton grew up in the nicest ways all of a sudden and Hacker just had to have it. So off they ran. Probably screwin' their way around the Caribbean or something. You're on vacation, right Hacker? You won't even be missed for a week or two. And we'll have a letter of resignation from Honie here, citing personal reasons. It'll play. People'll snicker and then forget all about you two."

"God, that's brilliant," Julie Warren breathed.

Harold Stilwell cleared his throat. "Uh, Wynnona, I'm not sure I understand …"

"Oh, you understand all right," Big Wyn said sarcastically. "You know exactly what's going on here. So here –" She thrust the shotgun at him. "Take 'em out to the swamps, shoot 'em, and make sure they go into a lagoon with a couple of hungry gators. We don't want any bodies floating up in a few weeks."

Harold took the gun and stared at it for a moment. Then he looked up at his wife.

"Wyn, honey, I can't …"

"Harold Stilwell," Wyn's voice thundered in the small motor home. "You will do as I say. I have spent the last twenty years taking care of your sorry ass. Everything you own I gave you. The food you eat, the clothes on your back, even this godforsaken piece of trash you live in…they are all mine. Ever since I took you away from that grease-monkey shop of yours, I have given you everything. I earned all the money. All you have ever been good for is doing what I told you to do. Without me, you'd still be a dumb hick living in nowhere, Indiana. So quit beating around the bush and do what I say."

His eyes teared suddenly, and he ducked his head in shame. "Wyn," he pleaded. "Don't make me."

"Goddam it!" she yelled, bending down and getting right in his face. "Did you hear what I just said? You are a worthless worm without me. Worthless! Now I'm not going to tell you again, you worm. Just suck it up and go do it. Do you hear? DO IT!"

Harold Stilwell stood up straight as if he had been jolted by lightening. His eyes were still wet, but he glanced down and jacked a shell into the chamber. The authoritative click sounded like a death knell to me.

Suddenly, the gun roared. Instinctively, I flinched and ducked and I saw Honie, across the table, jump at the sound.

Harold Stilwell held the shotgun pointed at the ample midsection of his wife. She was looking at him with a puzzled expression. She stood there, unmoving, for a long moment while the smell of cordite filled the little motor home. Then, as if in slow motion, she crumpled, wordless, to the floor.

Julie Warren, who had been standing and grinning against the far wall, sprang forward with a cry. "What the...! Wyn! WYN?" She pulled Big Wyn Stilwell over onto her back. Wyn's midsection was a mass of spattered blood. "You killed her!" Julie yelled furiously at Harold, her spit spraying. "You killed her! Goddam it! You ..."

She took a half step towards Harold. The gun roared a second time and Julie Warren's face disintegrated in a horrifying spray of red mist. The ceiling, the walls and Honie and I were instantly covered with a film of blood and tissues from Julie's exploding head. As her lifeless body tumbled to the floor, I fought down the bile that rose quickly in my throat. Across the table, Honie whimpered once and fainted.

Only now did Harold Stilwell move. He slowly stepped over the two bodies, reached into the storage locker from which the shotgun had come, and pulled out a handful of fresh shells.

"No, Harold, don't" I begged. "There's been enough killing her tonight."

If he heard me, he didn't react. He calmly broke the shotfun open, popped out the spent, smoking shells and thumbed two fresh rounds into the magazine, he clicked the gun closed again and pumped them into the chamber. Slowly he turned, the gun pointing in front of him, until he was facing me.

"Harold, please," I said. "Shoot me if you have to, but don't shoot the girl. She's got her whole life in front of her."

Harold never said a word. His eyes were gray and dead and empty. He raised the gun, turned it around and tucked the barrel under his chin.

"No!" I yelled frantically. "No! No! No!"

The gun roared for a third and final time.

TWENTY-SIX

I t was almost midmorning before someone showed up. It was Charley Dillon, the Doral maintenance man who was a friend of Harold's, who finally stopped by to share a cup of coffee and swap some engine stories with Harold. His old pal was mostly faceless and splattered against the wall of his motor home.

Sticking his head in the door of the motor home, Charley also saw the bodies of Big Wyn and Julie Warren, a semicomatose Honie and me. I was sitting on my bench, hands bound behind my back.

"Good morning," I said when his horrified face reflected the carnage he saw. "I'd appreciate it if you would untie me first and then call the cops."

He untied my hands second. First he blew his breakfast all over the ground outside the RV. I figured it had been six or seven hours that I had been sitting there. Six or seven hours with three dead people and one young and innocent victim. Six or seven hours with nothing to do but look at graphic death and think about things. Like evil. Life choices. Unhappiness. Life and death.

Strangely perhaps, I found myself thinking more about Harold Stilwell than his famous golfing wife. I knew that Big Wyn's story would get the most play in the news reports inevitably to follow. Famous golf star blown away by her deranged husband. Tragedy on the links! An American hero-ine meets an untimely end. I could almost hear Jack Whitaker doing one of his wordy essays on the tube, waxing poetic about "death be not proud," or some such nonsense.

No, Wynnona's life and death was not interesting to me, sitting there all that night in the trailer of death. There are lots of Big Wyns in this day and age. They might not be sports stars and media darlings and they usually don't end up lying crumpled in a bloody heap...but they are out there. They are the businessmen who like to manage using fear as the primary motivational tool. They are the husbands and sometimes the wives who exact some measure of revenge against the helplessness of living in this modern world by making miserable the lives of all those close around. They are the pool-hall bullies with the meaty fists and the college professors with the smarmy repartee. They are all those who are not happy unless the world is remade to their liking, and that's such an impossible job that they are rarely, if ever, happy.

No, I spent that long night and morning thinking about Harold, the little guy who had finally had enough. That doesn't happen often enough. The little guys like Harold are used to taking abuse, putting up with the bullying, making the best of it, shrugging their shoulders and putting their best foot forward.

Like most of the little guys, Harold did not demand much. He wanted peace and quiet, some time to do some fishing, perhaps a little respect in place of affection. But even those small demands are too much for the Big Wyns of the world, who are threatened by any demand which does not originate with or have a direct bearing upon themselves.

Harold's story would not play in the media, I knew. The little guys are rarely, if ever, heard. That's why they're little guys. He would be remembered as that crazy guy who blew away that famous golf lady. Not as a man abused for years who finally had enough and did something. Even if it was a drastic something.

I remembered Wyn's phrase when I had confronted her with the known truths in her windowed suite of rooms. *A bunch of damn mumbo jumbo.* Sitting there amid all the expired lives oozing blood onto the floor of Harold's trailer home, that phrase kept coming back to me. In fact, it was what Harold had said when I suggested that he didn't have to live his life under Wyn's thumb. It was what Wyn had said when she realized that her house of cards was about to come crashing down on her. *A bunch of damn mumbo jumbo.*

After sitting helpless in that trailer for five or six hours, watching three bodies cool, I realized it was the perfect summation of what life is all about. *A bunch of damn mumbo jumbo.*

I felt badly for Harold and for all the other little guys in the world. It stayed with me for the next day or two, while I was floating in and out of interviews with the police and the media and the police again. I kept it to myself, bottled up inside, and instead simply reported the events as they had happened. I did my job.

The headlines were screamers, including the one over the story I filed with my editor in Boston. He thought it was good enough to copyright and enter for some big national reporting prize. I told him I thought that was all a bunch of damn mumbo jumbo. After all, my account was just a factual report of events. It said nothing about the little guys having taken about as much as they could take.

The final round of the tournament was cancelled and for a few days, it appeared that the future of the Ladies Professional Golf Association was in some doubt as well. With both the commissioner and the chairman of the player's council murdered, followed by a flood tide of scandal and rumor — Casey Carlyle was arrested as an accessory for the murder of Benton Bergmeister — the idea of continuing to play a game seemed suddenly irrelevant. Honie Carlton was treated for shock and seemed to be doing well back in the hospital. But she would, no doubt, have nightmares for years to come.

I was inundated with requests to spill everything I knew to all the network news and talk shows and the gossip tabloids. Since I could never tell the difference between the two, I declined to be interviewed by either one. Monday afternoon, I was packing my bags and beginning to think longingly again of my quiet and peaceful little beach shack on the bluff above the sea, where I could be alone and think. The telephone range. It was Mary Beth Burke.

"Hacker," she said. "Some of the girls and I have been meeting and we've reached some decisions and we want you to be the first to hear them. Can you come down?"

I went. I figured the immediate prospects for the Tour were pretty bleak. Sponsors would probably withdraw in droves, clubs would cancel their contracts and the TV boys would be running hellbent for the hills to avoid this juicy sex scandal. The LPGA could expect excellent coverage from the supermarket tabloids for months to come.

In the hotel meeting room, most of the Tour's big-name players were seated around a long table. Patty Sheehan, Betsy King, Rosie Jones, Nancy Lopez, Pat Bradley and a few others. Sybil Montgomery was there, and Mary Beth Burke appeared to be chairing the whole thing. They all looked curiously at me when I walked in and sat down.

"Hacker,' Burkey said, "We've been having a real cat fight in here for the last few hours, but we've scratched it out and come to some agreements."

I looked around the table. I could see on their faces that the discussion had been both candid and brutal.

"We've all agreed that the one thing that's most important to us is that we keep playing golf," Burkey said. "All of us in here, and I'm sure just about every girl on the Tour, agree that playing the game is what we're all about. The money, the glory, the fame and fortune stuff is all well and good, but it ain't worth shit if you can't play the game."

She looked around the table and seemed to draw strength from the nods of agreement she saw.

"Now, we ain't stupid and we know that there's an awful long road ahead of us," she continued. "We're gonna lose sponsors, we're gonna lose tournaments, we're gonna lose TV money. Hell, even the golf-ball people might not give us range balls!" There was laughter all around. "But we've finally agreed this morning that we don't give a rat's ass! We're gonna dig our hells in the dirt and keep on playing. If it turns out we have to play for a hundred bucks first place money in some bohicket muni in front of seven people and a dog...well by damn, we're gonna do it. Because that's what's important...playing the game. We figure once people understand that we're serious, they'll come back to watch."

Mary Beth looked around the table again.

"This time, we're gonna run the show the right way," she continued. "Everyone in this room is gonna be responsible. We've held our first election already, and our lil ole British princess has been officially selected and duly sworn in as our new head bitch!"

Sybil gazed at me with eyes bright and alive and proud.

"So that's about it," Mary Beth concluded. "We just wanted you to hear about this because of all you went through in the last few days, and we hope that you'll see fit to give us another chance to prove ourselves some point down the road."

It was my turn to study the faces of the famous golf professionals gathered around the conference table. I saw resolve and determination and pluckiness. I saw also peace and that new-found inner power that belongs only to those little guys who decided to stop being little guys.

I stood up.

"When you get things straightend out and put on your first tournament, call me," I said. "I'll be there. And I'll even pay my own way!"

They hooted and laughed as I turned away and headed for home.

.

THE END